SHOWDOWN AT
CRAZY MAN CREEK

Eskiminzin's Aravaipa tribe had been brutally attacked by white men, and reprisals were inevitable. Scout Linus Buckthorn was sent out from Camp Sweeton to warn the settlers. But he found Alvaro Galvo's family already slaughtered, Lady Amanda Fairfax wandering alone, and three-year-old Lucy Marsden in the ruins of her family's homestead. With his charges, Buckthorn, found himself surrounded on an island in the middle of a creek, awaiting the attack of Broken Nose, the Aravaipa sub-chief.

ELLIOT LONG

SHOWDOWN AT CRAZY MAN CREEK

Complete and Unabridged

LINFORD
Leicester

First published in Great Britain in 1992 by
Robert Hale Limited
London

First Linford Edition
published 1996
by arrangement with
Robert Hale Limited
London

British Library CIP Data

Long, Elliot
    Showdown at Crazy Man Creek.—Large print ed.—
    Linford western library
    1. English fiction—20th century
    I. Title II. Series
    823.9'14 [F]

    ISBN 0–7089–7879–7

Published by
F. A. Thorpe (Publishing) Ltd.
Anstey, Leicestershire

Set by Words & Graphics Ltd.
Anstey, Leicestershire
Printed and bound in Great Britain by
T. J. Press (Padstow) Ltd., Padstow, Cornwall

This book is printed on acid-free paper

1

THERE was something wrong, Alvaro Galvo suddenly realized. Not with the homestead, but the land. Its morning vibrance was missing. It was too quiet.

He was standing by the well, some thirty yards from the *casa*. Though he could see no reason out there for his disquiet, he fidgeted nervously with the wooden bucket in his hand.

He shaded his eyes with his right hand and stared momentarily at the dawn sun. Its golden orb was beginning to climb above the hills ahead of him. Over the years he had always thought those hills yonder — freely greened with vegetation — looked more like crumpled peaks of brown paper in this early light.

And normally he would have rejoiced in the view — and the warming rays that struck his swarthy face, ironing out the care-worn hollows in it. But for some strange, inexplicable reason, not this morning. There was an unusual, odd quiet pervading it. And he noticed: no birds sang.

To his left his burro brayed and shuffled restlessly at its tether under the lean-to. Involuntarily he turned startled eyes to look at it. Too, he noticed now, the pigs in the pen were squealing more than they normally did. A couple were standing up, snorting, their forelegs resting on the stout fence, their small eyes staring out towards the west. Only the chickens appeared to be behaving naturally. Maybe that was because he had just let them out of their coop. They were clucking and scratching at the worn ground in front of the adobe homestead.

Again Alvaro allowed his brown gaze to stare around the vast, harsh land; the land from which he had wrenched his living these past fifteen years. He could see nothing unusual.

Nothing at all.

But despite his efforts to reassure himself, his senses kept insisting that things weren't right. And, he realized now, the hackles on his neck were beginning to prickle up uncomfortably; realized that his flesh was beginning to crawl. And there was another thing, too. The house dogs weren't rushing to greet him and fuss about him as they usually did.

He turned and stared at the green, steeple hills to the west now, feeling he must inevitably see *something*. But, as they had always done, they stood innocent and warm and calm in the dawn sun. They didn't seem to carry any threat at all.

He licked his dry lips. *So why did he feel so strange?* Why did he feel that some terrible thing was stalking the land?

Striving desperately to shrug off his discomfort he tied the bucket to the rope on the capstan over the well and slowly lowered it until he could hear it splash and sink with a gurgle into the water.

Then he saw the body. At first he didn't believe what he was seeing. Then he wondered why he had not seen it before.

It was his fifteen-year-old son, Felipe.

But now, as if to mask the horror of what he was observing, he realized a ridiculous disbelief was fighting to take over his mind. Horror-struck he turned away. It was not Felipe he saw there. It was a trick of the light. Yes, it was dark there. The bundle was something somebody had left there. He would have a word with Mama about it.

But he knew he was fooling himself. Yet, still, he couldn't allow himself to believe what he saw.

Felipe was on the hills, with the sheep on night watch. He, Alvaro, had instructed his son to carry out the duty last night, along with the dogs. It couldn't be him lying there.

Now Alvaro wondered if this could be some terrible nightmare; that he would suddenly wake up in bed with Mama and find the vision gone. But he realized now his mind was trying to crawl into some form of surreal world; that it was trying to drive the truth of what he had just seen into some hidden corner of it.

He wanted to swamp the vision. Bury it. Try to imagine he hadn't seen what he had. But he found the stark image wouldn't go away. That it was far worse than anything his mind, even at its most nightmarish, could ever conjure up.

Forcing himself, against the great reluctance to do so, he turned again to look at his son. He was propped against the fence that penned the pigs. Alvaro could see that he had no hair on the top of his head. All there was was a bloody patch. His brown, naked body was a mass of small wounds. Flies feasted on the ripped flesh. More horrible still, his genitals were burned black, as though he had been sat and forcefully made to suffer the glowing, fiercely-hot embers of a fire as they ate at him. Alvaro could see the concentration of horrendous pain his son must have endured, frozen on his face, fixed there by death.

Then Alvaro saw the dogs he had wondered about. They were scattered about his son. Bloody. Arrow stuck. Slashed. Broken. Dead.

Alvaro could not stop the wailing cry that escaped him. His eyes became wild before he whispered, "*Madre de Dios!*" He crossed himself.

He knew the boy's mutilations could mean only one thing: APACHE!

Like a cold, creeping stream, dread began to seep into him. He found his anxieties were beginning to rise ten-fold. Almost rigid with fear now, he allowed his gaze to re-examine the land, at the same time crossing himself again and begging all the saints and the Holy Mother for protection and to accept Felipe to them, though unconfessed.

And suddenly, as if galvanized, he

began to haul quickly on the well-rope. His anguish-driven thoughts were now searching swiftly for some life-saving strategy that would keep himself and the rest of his family from a terrible death.

The house was strong; it could withstand an attack. Also, if the siege was to be a long one they would need plenty of water in the house. That was why he had to stand here and wind up the bucket. Maybe the Apache would get tired of trying to reach them, break off and take the livestock and leave them in peace.

Now he realized his bladder was not retaining fluid any more. That he had lost control of himself. That urine was running down his leg. Distressed and revolted by it, he listened to the squeaking of the capstan handle. *Madre de Dios*. It sounded like a scream in the bright morning. He had been intending for weeks to grease it!

He was thinking even more desperately now: once he got to the house, to his gun, to Mama, to Esteban, to Carlos, to Alicia, to Carmelita, to . . .

Shockingly, he felt the first war-arrow embed itself in his chest. The second, in his stomach. The third alongside it, plumb into the belly-button.

With a harsh, despairing cry he let go of the capstan handle. He dropped to the ground, gasping with the sudden pain. Shock momentarily drove all control from his limbs. He heard the screech of the capstan as it unwound, the bucket splash back into the water in the well.

Now driven by fear for his family's safety he quickly recovered. He began to crawl on all-fours. He could feel the feathered ends of the arrows scraping painfully across the stony, hard-packed ground. He could see the soil was becoming bloody now with his own gore.

"Mama!" he shouted hoarsely in his native Spanish. "Apache! Save yourself. The children . . ."

Blood flooded into his throat and mouth, gushed to the earth.

Now he could see Esteban. The boy appeared at the open doorway of the *casa*. As soon as his son saw him his fourteen year old face became wide-eyed, his face warped with alarm. Alvaro could see the boy had his machete in his hand and appeared prepared to use it.

Before he could cry a warning, Alvaro watched the first arrow bury itself in the boy's neck. Watched the next bite into his son's stomach. Watched the blood spout redly from the boy's wounds. Then he heard his son's gurgling cry as he staggered back inside the dwelling.

Now, raking his very soul, Alvaro heard the screams from his wife and daughters and sons start up inside the house.

But he felt weak. He realized all his strength was draining redly from him on to the packed earth. He slumped and rolled over on to his back. He started to tremble. He was conscious of blood running from his mouth, down the side of his face. He could hear it splashing on to the parched earth near his right ear.

It was as though he was in a dream again, that reality had finally left him. Like phantoms he could see the Apache warriors moving past him now. They were familiar — dark, wiry men with long black hair. They wore their usual loincloths, doeskin leggings, coloured shirts and sweat bands round their raven locks. Some wore vests of leather or cloth. One had a battered army campaign hat on his head.

Alvaro rolled on to his side. "No, *señors*," he pleaded. "No."

He realized the only sound there really was coming from his mouth was the gurgle of his own blood drowning his vocal cords and lungs.

He lay there, trying to speak. Now he became aware that one of the braves had paused beside him. The Apache was looking down at him. Alvaro was surprised to see it was Broken Nose, an Aravaipa sub-chief he knew. He had traded with him on infrequent occasions.

He rolled on to his back again, staring at him. Alvaro could see no pity in the swarthy face.

He tried looking appealingly into the glittering, obsidian eyes. But he found the glare he met was devoid of emotion. All it was, was a cauldron of black hate.

Even so, Alvaro fumbled for words. Something that would appeal to Broken Nose. Something Alvaro thought might save his family.

"Broken Nose!" He gagged on his own blood, but persisted. "We have been friends. I have welcomed you to my house. You have drank at my well. Eaten my food. I beg of you, spare my children!"

As he made his noises he could now hear the screams inside the adobe and he rolled his head despairingly in his own gore. His emotions were now torn to ribbons, his riven anxiety complete.

11

Then Alvaro saw Carlos come staggering out of the doorway. He could see his son's entrails were hanging out of his stomach; could see crimson was pouring from the wound in a flood. The boy was holding out a twelve-year-old hand tremblingly towards him.

Alvaro's cry of horror and despair was an agonized exclamation mark on the still, beautiful morning.

But now, feeling old and empty and helpless, Alvaro watched the boy collapse. Watched as he sprawled into the dust inches from him to lie writhing on the ground, shrieking his agony.

Alvaro reared in an attempt to reach his youngest boy. But he heard Broken Nose's guttural, warning snarl above him. Then Alvaro felt the hard thumping blow crash on to his head.

His impressions were now of a vast darkness beginning to flood in on him, the screams of his son ringing in his ears.

Alvaro decided now his life had not been pure enough. Decided that his indiscretions with other women and a little banditry in younger days had caught up with him. And, because of it, he was now entering the very Gates of Hell.

★ ★ ★

Linus Buckthorn had had the ribbon of black smoke, reeding into the blue sky, in his sights some while now. His long, lantern-jawed face lengthened. It had to be Galvo's place, he thought. Restlessly his grey eyes surveyed the tree-studded hills around him.

The news about the slaughter of Eskiminzin's Aravaipas had come into Camp Sweeton four days ago. It had hit it like a bomb-shell.

Buckthorn knew a band of them had been settled peacefully for some time alongside the Aravaipa Creek, below Fort Grant. Knew that Lieutenant Royal E. Whitman, commander of the fort, after much negotiation, had befriended the Aravaipas and had

13

won their trust. He had persuaded Eskiminzin and his tribe to give up their arms, settle down and grow corn and cut grass to make hay to supply the fort.

Buckthorn blinked. Now such good work was in ruins. Even though the peace that sound men were trying to establish in this land would have meant he'd eventually lose his job as scout for the army, the bloody massacre of the Aravaipas only disgusted him. He didn't want to prolong earning his living on the basis of that kind of thing.

But the story had taken some believing at first. It was that a force of Americans, Mexicans and Christian Papago Indians from Tucson had attacked Eskiminzin's sleeping village early in the morning of April 30th 1871 . . . five days ago.

Buckthorn blinked at the brassy sky, the lines of his face hard and bitter. But it had been true enough.

And the story went that most

of the dead had been women and children. That they had been mercilessly slaughtered as they tried to flee.

Buckthorn shook his head. He still found it hard to believe. He knew it had been government policy through the army lately to placate the Apaches, talk to them, make treaties with them, get them to give up their murderous ways and they had been succeeding. So this white attack had sure upset the applecart, sent the whole thing rolling back to barbarism again.

Buckthorn narrowed his eyelids. He also knew, had a solid suspicion anyway, that too many men in Tucson were making a lot of money out of the Indian wars, so it would be bad business if they stopped . . .

Swamping his thoughts on the matter, for he knew he was a very small piece of meat in a very big stewpot, Buckthorn eased his roan to a halt and dismounted, just below the ridge top he'd been riding under cover of. He had a job to do.

15

He bellied up to the rimrock. With patient scrutiny he surveyed the rocky land flattening out below him towards the greenery by the river. He could see Galvo's unattended sheep dotted the hillside.

Then a cold hand clutched at Buckthorn's gut as he saw his worst fears were confirmed. Yes, it was the Mexican's *casa* that had been torched.

Bitterly, he allowed his gaze to rove over the arid land around him. There was no movement. Above him the noon sun was a brassy ball. He'd never fully get used to the heat in this Godforsaken land. It was like living in a cauldron. A fiery sandwich.

He felt the hot sand beneath him, scorching through his buckskins. Felt the scorching rays above him, burning his back. And all the time the sweat seeped from him.

He sighed, distaste in him for the task ahead.

He had to go down there. See what he could do. He needed water. The water in Galvo's well was known for its sweet quality. Galvo was famed for his hospitality, too. Mexican food had always made a swell change from hardtack, beans and bacon. He stared at the vultures, circling in the brassy vault above and flopping on the ground around the burnt-out *casa*. Seemed that little pleasure had come, savagely, to an end.

It caused him to compress his wide, grim, lipless mouth. With a little more trust at Camp Sweeton maybe this could have been avoided.

The new camp commander, Captain Vincent Fuller, had asked him as soon as the news had broken, to ride out to warn the settlers, miners and ranchers known to be in the vicinity, of almost certain Apache trouble.

Buckthorn blinked. Well, he'd tried. He had asked Fuller why not the White Mountain Apache scouts attached to the fort, too? The captain had been frank. He had explained he couldn't bring himself to ask them to undertake the duty until he knew them better.

Buckthorn had heard of Fuller's distrust of the Indian scouts attached to the army. It had preceded him. It had been fully proved now by his point-blank refusal.

Buckthorn looked skywards, watched the vultures some more. Well, Fuller's intractability had sure as hell put paid to Galvo's chances; his thoughts silently fumed, he was damn well sure of that.

Oh, he had continued to argue with Fuller. Had explained to him the men were completely trustworthy, but the captain had been adamant. Buckthorn spat. Even then he hadn't given in. He knew speed in warning the settlers was crucial if they were to save lives.

He had gone on to suggest sending a couple of troopers with the Apaches; that way an eye could be kept on them, if that was what was bothering him.

Buckthorn blinked as he recalled Fuller's answer. He had said curtly he couldn't afford them. That that was why he was having to send himself,

Buckthorn, out alone. The camp was depleted enough. He had a force out on patrol to the south as it was. No, it would have to be down to him and that was the end of the matter.

Buckthorn sighed. Had Fuller not been so chary, he conjectured now, maybe Galvo and his family would still be alive, assuming they were dead, that is. Buckthorn accepted he had yet to prove that. But he was a ninety-nine per cent certain of it in his own mind.

He had managed to warn the ones settled along Hernando's Creek, and what miners he had met in the hills. Alvaro Galvo's place was his last call. The one farthest out. It had taken three days of tortuous travel to reach here.

Now he pulled out his binoculars.

He had blackened the brass so that it didn't glint in the sun. He tried to keep the lens from mirroring the light and flashing off them. He'd got to be quite an expert at it, knowing a glint from them was like a beacon to the hostile, watching eye.

Patiently he made a detailed study of the land around. Whoever had visited Galvo's place had now gone. That was obvious by the vultures and his own observations.

That confirmed, he stowed the binoculars, climbed into the saddle on the roan, went over the ridge and eased his way down through the rocks and scrub. All around him, dotted amongst the sparse vegetation, giant saguaros stood like sentinels.

Now he saw some of Galvo's sheep cropping the grass, irrigated and greened up by the stream a mile away from the homestead.

As he rode into the area of Galvo's homestead, what he found sickened him. Even though he was no stranger to Apache depravations, he'd never get used to them. It was immediately obvious that Galvo's daughters and wife had been raped repeatedly before they had been savagely killed.

And he found the men had been

just butchered where they stood, apart from Felipe, still propped against the pigsty fence where he had obviously been placed for Galvo to see.

He drove off the glutted vultures with savage kicks.

Now, cold rage in him, Buckthorn cast his icy stare over the adobe *casa*. It was just a smouldering shell. The pigs had been butchered and taken, so had the chickens. Galvo's burro must had been taken along, too.

From the tracks around, Buckthorn estimated about fifteen Apaches. The arrows told him they were Aravaipa.

That didn't surprise Buckthorn overmuch, either. One thing, though, was sure: the Apaches would eat well for the next few days.

He took off his buckskin coat; found a small spade. He began to break the hard earth.

It took him until an hour before sunset to accomplish the task of burying the eight bodies. By the time he had finished his doeskin leggings were sweat-sodden; near white where they had dried.

It had been a shallow hole. He had piled rocks over the bodies to stop the coyotes from getting at them. He drove in a crude cross and scratched THE GALVOS on it with the point of his skinning knife.

Now he spat and wiped his streaming brow and stared at the blue sky.

He could have ridden away. Left them to nature. But that wouldn't have been the act of a Christian man, he reckoned. Though he had no strong feelings about the faith; he just did what he felt was the decent thing.

He crossed to the well now to fill his canteens. As he peered over the stone lip, he reared back. The well was already stinking. A second look told him the Apaches had thrown the dogs into it.

However, he decided, despite having no water, he could risk a fire, fire being already here.

After a meal of beans and bacon

and coffee made from the last of his water he swung up on to the roan and headed into the sunset. He knew where water was. And he would have to head for it.

But it was only minutes later he had to draw in rein fast, his gut tightening. Face grim he eased his mount into the cover of the crumbling pillar of rock he was passing.

Now he saw a banner of dust rising above the ridge a mile ahead. And he had little doubt; it had to be Apache dust. Though it was unusual for them to raise so much.

2

BUCKTHORN dismounted and waited, studying the swirling dust. He flicked a brief glance at the sky — now shot with red, yellow and purple streamers of high cloud, stained by the last rays of the sun. He could see its red orb was sinking behind the sawtooth mountains, the foothills of which he was beginning to climb into now.

He watched the dust banner move north-west. By the size of it, it couldn't be a big party that made it, he decided. At the most three riders, maybe less.

And he wasn't full certain it had been made by Apaches. There was too much of it. The Apache moved stealthily, choose what he did. But reason told him it more than likely was them. After what had recently been done to them, the Aravaipas would be stomping these mountains like packs of crazy timber-wolves.

And they wouldn't be caring too much who knew it, he reckoned. Buckthorn knew the Apache was fully aware the army took time to muster, get organized. And any big, cumbersome army patrols they encountered they usually evaded and outstripped easily in this inhospitable country. But, if the chase did get too hot, too determined, the Apache would, and usually did, run south to their old strongholds in the mountains of Mexico. Move over the magic line the white man had drawn, but couldn't cross. The border.

Buckthorn stared around the vast, rocky country, red in the sunset. He was just one slightly anxious man in a big, hostile land. And, at rock bottom, what was truly the only thing strong inside him at the moment, was his instinct for self-preservation: the need to get out of this present situation alive. He'd wait for that dust to clear the area before he moved again.

He pulled out the piece of wood he was currently whittling at. He held it up admiringly for a moment. It was beginning to take on the form of the striking owl he intended, its talons reaching for a yet to be carved mouse. His skinning knife began its patient work.

* * *

It was full dark before he decided to move again. First he read the stars, found the way west, and struck out for Camp Sweeton. He travelled for three hours, watched the moon come up and rise steadily.

Choose what, he decided, he needed sleep and his horse needed rest. Both of them had had precious little of either these past two days. And he knew a place ideal for both.

He found the pleasant glade he'd been heading for. It was faintly silvered by the quarter moon. He was glad to see the small stream still tumbled down the rocks to feed the lush grass and trees at the end of the deep gully. Sometimes it ran dry, he knew.

In the trees he hobbled the roan, gave her a nosebag of oats, filled his canteens and settled down with a hunk of dry bread and jerky, followed by a handful of gritty raisins.

Half an hour later Buckthorn was settling to sleep. His now grazing horse lifted its head and snorted bringing Buckthorn back to alert erectness. Then he heard the faint crack of a branch up the gully. Even above the chuckle of the water it sounded like a pistol shot in the still night.

He moved immediately. He slipped the hobbles off the horse and led her away. Now, fifty yards from his original position, he crouched low. Breath held, he listened again.

He heard another noise. A dislodged stone this time. It clattered harshly.

Couldn't be Apache, Buckthorn asserted in his own mind to alleviate his slight puzzlement. They never made that much noise in a year. But whoever it was who was skulking about out there could be arousing every critter and maybe every Apache within a mile around.

In a patch of thick, tall brushwood, he tied the mare. He hoisted his long, slim skinning knife. He knew it was razor-sharp. He honed it daily, religiously. It was handy for flaying hides, or cutting throats. And he had no qualms about using it for either. And he had practised both during his time in this harsh, uncompromising territory. And, all else aside, the plain truth was he couldn't do with noise at the moment, whoever was causing it. Not the way things were with Eskiminzin's Aravaipas.

He saw the indistinct, shadowy form now, a hundred yards up the gully. It was faintly silhouetted in the light of the moon. It was scrambling awkwardly down the rocky side of the deep gash in the hillside.

With swift, silent, ghostly movements

he got round behind. He could hear a cussing now. It sounded female. The dress looked fancy female, too. But he could not take any chances. If it was a squaw, there could be braves . . .

He came up behind her silently. He grabbed the long, dark, flowing hair that hung loosely from her bare head and jerked it back. He brought the knife down swiftly to draw it across the Adam's apple, then hesitated.

Upon a further, rapid examination he was astounded to see the pale, refined features of a white woman. A fancy white woman, too, in a fancy dress.

Before he could recover from his surprise she shrieked and he felt her start to fight against him.

With an anxious, angry growl he clamped his grubby left hand across her mouth, gagging her. Fiercely he dragged her down on to the rocky ground. He dropped on top of her, pressing his 184 pounds of sinewy muscle against her, pinning her to the gully side.

Now he glowered intensely around the moon-silvered ravine, searching for other movement.

None.

Now he could feel her writhing under him, still trying to scream. He could feel the slim shapely body jerking, pulsating against him.

"Damn it, woman," he hissed. "Be quiet."

Angrily he looked down into her big, defiant eyes which were staring up at him over his gnarled, not very clean, hand. It was hard to tell their colour in the silver dark. But they were blinking and glaring angrily at him.

When she saw he was male and white, she stopped struggling and went quiet.

"Better," he grunted, his voice barely a whisper.

He eased his hand off her mouth. The move revealed generous, sensuous lips.

"Who the hell are you?" he hissed.

"I am Lady Amanda Fairfax," she

blurted haughtily, angrily and loudly and demanded, "Get off me."

Buckthorn thought, Lady? That was a high-flown handle for this corner of the territory.

But, far from having any compunction to comply with her demand, he snarled quietly, "Damn it, keep your voice low." He glowered fiercely down at her. "Now, what the hell are you doin' blunderin' around at night like this in Apache country?"

Buckthorn realized the woman's eyes were blazing up at him now with a look that could only be interpreted as loathing disdain; as though he was something beneath her dignity to answer.

Anger coiled through him. Who the hell did the woman think she was? She was looking at him as though she was inspecting something that had crawled out from under a stone.

"I have been riding in the hills," she finally said, in a clipped, precise way. "My horse threw me and bolted," she went on after a pause. She pouted. "I have been trying to get back to my husband's camp. Though I'm sure, by now, he will have somebody out searching for me."

The lingo: Buckthorn was finding it hard to understand. Then he realized where he had heard it before. One or two officers, fresh out from that military school back East, West Point, sometimes talked like it, he recalled.

But beyond that, it was what she said, he thought grimly. Astonishment and disbelief flooded in on him. Then he speculated: had it been this woman who had made all the dust he had seen before sunset? Jesus, if it was . . . she had to be crazy, or her husband was. Maybe they both were.

But he found he had to bury the immediate contemptuous opinions he had of her for he could hardly believe what he was hearing. She'd been riding in the hills? As if it was Sunday afternoon at Fort Apache?

So incredible was it, it took him

a second or two to realize the full implications of what she had said. Now he spat sidewise to express his disdain, his angry thoughts demanding: was the damned woman trying to be funny?

He stared down at her. She was still glaring up at him as if revolted by him. And now she struggled.

Buckthorn held her in an iron grip. He ignored her struggles and her withering look. Instead he thought incredulously what kind of a man would let his wife do such a stupid thing as ride out in the hills, things being the way they were?

"You know Eskiminzin's Aravapais are loose?" he grated harshly now, his disbelief complete.

The woman now suddenly calmed and looked at him coolly and archly. "If you mean the native people . . ." She lifted her fine nose. "We have nothing to do with them."

"The *native* people?" Buckthorn growled. He was becoming more amazed by the second. "You have nothin' to do with them? What the hell you talkin' about, woman?" he demanded.

The fancy female stared at him as if surprised by his reaction. "It's better to not mix." She pouted her now firm, though sensuous, lips. "We never mixed with them in India, or Africa. You have to let them know their place. It's better for everybody."

Buckthorn blinked. He was finding it difficult to understand the woman. Let the Apaches know their place? Damn it, they knew that right enough. It was here. And they frequently killed people to prove it.

Bemused, Buckthorn shook his head, causing his unkempt, sun-blonded locks, hanging from under his grey stetson, to wipe across the fringed buckskin coat covering his shoulders.

He rubbed his unshaven jaw and spat again, ignoring the female's loathing glare as he did so.

He was still having difficulty understanding the woman, and what she said. Maybe the sun had got to her? It sent people a little crazy sometimes. And what or where was this India and Africa she was babbling on about? He thought he knew most of the important places west of here, clear to California. Seems he was lacking a little knowledge there. Maybe they were places back East? He found a little comfort in that. Sure, that made a bit of sense. He'd never been there.

"Hell, ma'am," he whispered. "You don't seem to understand. You could get killed out here. The Apache is on the warpath."

She had continued to glare up at him. "If you will allow me to rise I will gladly explain," she said. She looked at him meaningly now. While she did she wrinkled her fine nose. "And when did you last have a bath?"

A bath? More contempt flooded through Buckthorn. Didn't the woman know water was a plumb scarce commodity hereabouts? And that it weakened a man to bathe too much,

35

anyway? But, that niggle aside, he was slightly embarrassed now to realize their positions. He got up off her and stood up.

She came to her feet quickly and stared at him. He saw she wore a beautiful suit made of some fine material. Buckthorn had only seen the like of it before on rare occasions. Usually gowns like that were worn by the senior officers' ladies at Fort Apache, or Tucson, places like that, when they went riding.

It comprised of a long split skirt, white blouse and a kind of small coat that fastened tight and neat around her slim waist. And Buckthorn had to admit he'd never seen a more pretty and well-formed female. She seemed to have the same arrogant spirit of a pure, thoroughbred Arab mare. The kind of wild knowledge they appeared to have of their quality. He'd only seen one of the breed once himself, but the experience had stuck firmly and forever in his mind and the impression it had made on him. And the memory fitted this woman to perfection.

"Now," she began indignantly dusting off her dress.

Half listening, because she was such a stunning looker, Buckthorn realized, now she was erect, she was almost as tall as himself. Five feet ten inches. In the moonlit dark he met the big, bold eyes that were level with his own.

She was saying scornfully, "The natives would not dare to attack us. My husband is Lord Algernon Fairfax. If our shooting party were molested in any way it would have far-reaching international repercussions. The strongest of representations would immediately be made by the British Ambassador to your President."

Faced with that mouthful Buckthorn shook his head, completely baffled by the talk now. Habitually, when puzzled and confused, he spat.

"Hell, to be honest, ma'am, I don't know what you're talkin' about. All I know is if we don't get out of these mountains purty quick we is liable to end up very dead."

"Nonsense," she snorted. "And I don't like men who swear."

She looked at him through the silver moonlight. Her expression, Buckthorn noticed, made it clear she didn't very much like what she saw. Buckthorn spat again when he realized it.

"Have you a camp near here?" she was demanding.

Buckthorn jerked his head slightly indicating to the rear. He was finding he was working up a high dislike for this female.

"Back a piece," he answered. "An' for Pete's sake, keep your voice down, ma'am."

But she continued to glare at him. "I am not 'ma'am'," she shouted. "I am Lady Fairfax. Kindly address me as such."

Buckthorn felt a quibble of anger stir in him. This had gone on far enough. Damn it, he didn't owe this woman a thing.

"You're what the hell I've a mind to call you," he growled. "Now get this straight, lady. You're nothin' to me. I could leave you here right now, an' truth be known, I've a mind to."

The woman tilted her head. Her fine chin-line etched itself creamily in the moonlight. Her skin was too fair and too white to have been in this country long, Buckthorn decided.

And she was now saying contemptuously, "That is the answer I have come to expect in this country. Clearly, you are as uncouth as most of the common rabble I have encountered here."

Buckthorn snorted, his anger flaring up. "Damn it, I know what you're sayin'. And I've a mind to spank your ass. You come mighty thin with the manners yourself."

An outraged gasp escaped the woman. "How dare you?" she remonstrated.

He glowered through the night at her. "I dare any damned thing I like, if it suits me. A man's his own man in this country. It's what he's capable of that counts, not the fancy title he holds. That's the bottom line out here, *ma'am*. And I don't take too much lip from a woman, either, no matter who she is. When I treat folk decent, I expect it to be returned."

Buckthorn attempted to cool his irate feelings. It was becoming obvious the woman knew nothing of the country or the etiquette that ruled it. Maybe where she came from, they did things differently. But here, with him, she'd sure as hell do it his way.

At the thoughts, he paused, brought up to a sudden halt by them. Damn it, distasteful as it was becoming, having found her, he'd have to take it upon himself to make sure she was returned safely to the camp of that damned-fool of a husband of hers. Why the man had allowed her to stray in the first place, he thought nastily, frankly took some hard understanding.

He looked at her. She was staring moodily, straight back at him.

"Mrs Fairfax," he began. He paused to find words she could maybe understand. "Whether you 'don't mix', as you put it, with the natives, is not the point. The point is we're in one hell of a fix here. Eskiminzin's Aravaipas are on the warpath. They're swarming in these mountains looking for trouble. They'll rape you an' use you soon as look at you if they catch up with you. They won't give a damn who you are, who your husband is, or where you come from. An' Washington will be unable to do a damned thing about it. Can't you get that into your pretty head?"

For the first time, he was glad to see Mrs Fairfax appeared hesitant.

"I don't understand," she returned. "We came here a fortnight ago to do business and some hunting. My husband was assured things were relatively peaceful. That the savages were subdued. What has happened?"

Buckthorn told her.

Again the haughty look came back. "But that is nothing to do with us," she declared. "We are not even American. We are English."

"To an Apache, ma'am, it won't matter a damn if you're sky-blue pink, you shouldn't be here. And the Aravaipas have been bad used by white men recently. So who you are or where you come from, won't matter a hoot in hell to him. He'll kill you where you stand."

"But, I'm a woman!"

"So were his squaws, an' their children, lyin' dead alongside the creek near Fort Grant, if it's true what I heard," he found himself blurting out.

Mrs Fairfax's imperious face lengthened. She went quiet, as if she was assessing what she had been told. There wasn't the disdain there now. She had clearly gone paler, too. Was the seriousness of their position getting through at last, Buckthorn wondered.

"Ma'am, I'll do all I can to get you back to your husband," he said with the quiet, though sometimes angry, voice he had maintained throughout the conversation. Even though Mrs Fairfax had not. "Are you and your husband all there is? If so, I will urge your husband to return with me to Camp Sweeton, along with yourself."

Again the chin came up, her fine, almost imperceptively hooked nose etched in the moonlight.

"What makes you think he'll listen to — to — " She thinned her lips. "Our entourage consists of Sir Stephan Greyford-Stuart and his wife, Lady Greyford-Stuart; also the Honourable Markland Lacy. There is Hepton, the butler — "

Buckthorn's ears pricked up. Butler? What the hell was that?

"And we have a guide by the name of Nathan Foley."

Buckthorn's eyebrows went up, forgetting the butler. "Nat?" he said.

My God, he thought with slight amusement, Nat had the silkiest tongue this side of the Rio Grande. And a keen eye for an easy buck. But Nat hadn't the most amazing ability as a guide.

Buckthorn had already got to thinking just who was guiding whom out there since the woman had mentioned Nat.

He knew Nat Foley could give an expert guided tour of the best saloons and whorehouses in the south-west, but the wastelands and mountains? No sir, that was another matter entirely.

"Do you know him?" Mrs Fairfax said. "He is quite a character."

Buckthorn nodded. He'd heard stronger words describe Nat. Used some himself on occasion.

"We've crossed trails, ma'am."

"You find him amusing?"

Buckthorn had found Nat, at times, to be purely a pain in the ass. He was still owed ten bucks from their last poker game played three months ago at Fort Apache.

He said, "Guess Nat has his moments."

He stared at her now, tired of the talk and *tired*. "Ma'am, I suggest some sleep. Then we'll look for your husband's camp come first light."

Buckthorn, being honest with himself, still wasn't relishing the prospect. It was a chore he could well do without. He had enough to be going on with preserving his own hide, leave aside that of some arrogant English female and maybe the party she was with. But he realized he had now come reluctantly around to accepting the situation he had become involved in.

Mrs Fairfax was saying, breaking his thoughts, "I could do with a warm meal. I haven't eaten since noon."

Buckthorn glanced at her. "I got bread, jerky an' water, some raisins."

She raised her fine eyebrows. "What is . . . jerky?"

"Dried meat."

Again she looked haughtily at him in the silver right before she toned the look down, perhaps because of his hard stare.

"Couldn't you cook something?" she said sharply, though quietly. "Surely you have beans, bacon, coffee. I've heard it's a common diet in these western parts." She tilted that chin again. "If it's payment you are worried about, don't be," she added. "Lord Fairfax will reimburse you handsomely." Buckthorn detected that note of arrogant disdain creep into her tone again in the last bit of her conversation.

"It isn't a matter of not wanting to, ma'am," he said, ignoring it. "Fire can be seen for miles, especially dark like it is. I have no plans on inviting the Aravaipas to supper. Fact is, I'm going to move away from here right now. Been too much noise."

Buckthorn heard an exasperated gasp leave the woman. "I think you are making wholly too much of this," she rebuked. "I frankly don't believe half of what you have said. I have met numerous common people with tall tales to tell, hoping they will be believed and that the rot they speak will advance their status, or, more likely, their wealth."

Again that warm anger fired in Buckthorn's stomach. "I don't give a damn for your opinions, Mrs Fairfax," he hissed. "It's jerky an' water tonight. But first of all, we're movin'." He grabbed her arm and began to lead her off down the hillside. "Now shut that damned sharp mouth of yours an' come on."

She shook herself free of him angrily. "I'll do no such thing."

Buckthorn had neither the time nor the patience for tantrums, least of all from this damned unpleasant woman. "Then stay here and die, Mrs Fairfax," he growled.

He went off down the gully towards his horse. Deliberately he didn't look back. He'd dealt with fractious mares before. Though not the human kind. But at the moment he didn't see a deal of difference. He undid the rein holding the roan. The mare snorted softly. He held her nose. "Damn it, I got enough noise with one flighty female."

He made off towards his night camp. He saddled the roan, secured the saddlebags and was lifting his canteens to hook on the saddle horn when he heard the noise behind him. It didn't alarm him. He knew it was the woman. He could hear her laboured breathing. It was half a mile of rough ground to the camp.

"You *are* prepared to leave me here, aren't you?" she said, her incredulity clear. "Despite the dangers you talk about."

"I've no time for silly female ways at the moment, ma'am," he cut back. "You either come or you don't. I won't have argument." He added firmly, "Get that into your head and things can only improve between us."

"How dare you!" Again she glared haughtily.

He could see, though it didn't bother him, she was plainly outraged by his bluntness. Her fine head was held high, her sensuous mouth compressed. Then she seemed to relent over something.

"I will not tell my husband of your behaviour," she breathed now. "If I did, he would, no doubt, horsewhip you."

That brought Buckthorn's head round with a jerk. He was finding it mighty hard to believe a lot of what was coming from this woman. But the threat had come with a plain truth he couldn't ignore.

He said slowly, icily, looking into her big, beautiful eyes, "A muleskinner tried that once, Mrs Fairfax," he said quietly. "They buried him two hours later, after they'd made a box for him. If you get to tellin' your husband about me, tell him that, too."

He grabbed her then, by her slim waist. She was surprisingly light. Before she could protest he put her up into the saddle. With supple agility he swung up behind her and put his hands under her arms and took the reins.

It was then he heard the yips of the coyotes, always present, were nearer than they had previously been. And, he wasn't sure the noises were made by those desert scavengers. Although it was almost imperceptible, he thought there was a slightly different timbre to their tone.

It sounded Apache.

Buckthorn set his long jaw and narrowed his steel-grey eyes. He urged the roan into the night.

3

BUCKTHORN angled south, taking a wide sweep, picking his trail with great care. He listened constantly to the night. Apart from the usual critter noises — nothing, other than the coyotes. They were singing west of him now and he was still doubtful about their authenticity.

Mrs Fairfax remained silent. But it stirred him some to feel her lithe body moving against him with the motion of the horse. There was a faint hint of fine perfume there, too, above the sweat-scents of her body.

After an hour of careful travel he stopped at the hideaway he had been heading for. He had used it before. It was under a long overhang of rock, part of a gouged-out dry ravine. He edged the roan down the tortuous trail to reach it. As he did, he felt the air get noticably warmer. But he knew it wouldn't last. It was only the residual left in the rocks. The desert night-cold would soon seep down.

Under the overhang he climbed down and helped Mrs Fairfax. As she reached the ground she sank down on to a rock ledge. He could see the strain now beginning to appear on her face, the tired, tense lines etched around her eyes and mouth.

In the dark he unsaddled and hobbled the horse. Then he gave the woman some biscuits and jerky and a canteen of water, plus a handful of resins.

He didn't comment. Just held them out. He felt uncompromising. She either took them, or she didn't. However, she looked too tired to protest. She took the food and began to bite on it with strong, even teeth. But she took no pains to hide her distaste from him.

He got out his blanket roll, opened it and spread it on the ground. "Here, ma'am," he said. "Use this. It can get mighty cold."

She stared at him, then the blanket, again without comment. He observed she now seemed a trifle stunned by the events that had overtaken her — enough to quieten her somewhat; dampen her spirit. Though he felt no inclination to rouse *that* again.

He said, as he hunkered down against a boulder, "I suggest you get some sleep after you've eaten, Mrs Fairfax."

With that he folded his arms, put his head in the bow of the saddle. Within moments he was breathing evenly, in deep sleep.

★ ★ ★

Buckthorn awoke cold and stiff. He got up immediately and loosened up his sinewy limbs. That done, his narrow gaze searched the ravine, his ears cocked for noise. The terrain was still and blue-cold in the early dawn light. And silent, but for a few flutings of birdsong.

He was surprised to observe Mrs Fairfax had not used his blanket. She was lying on her right side, curled up, her arms wrapped across her chest. He could see her hands were tucked under her armpits for warmth.

He glowered at her, slightly angered. If she was too damn fine to accept his blanket, he wished to hell she'd let him know. He sure as hell wasn't. He could have had a more comfortable night than he'd had. There seemed to be no pleasing this woman.

He snorted his disapproval. His stare was long upon her before he walked out from under the huge overhang and climbed up the ravine side to the top of the steep rise.

Bellied on the rim of the ravine he ranged his binoculars over the hilly land. The sun was already pinking the tops of the mountains to the north, that rose majestically above the foothills. Down here, though, the folds of the brown hills were, at the moment, pale blue, the patches of vegetation dark-green in the half-light.

It was then he saw the smoke rising. It was like a black, moving scar cut into the pink background of the mountains. It was maybe five miles away, north-west. A chill cold wrapped his body. Was it the camp of the people Mrs Fairfax was with? he wondered. From what he'd heard and observed through her, only they would be stupid enough to build a fire as big as that.

But, again, what was Nathan Foley doing letting them? Even Nat had enough savvy to know that that was a damned stupid thing to do in this country. But, if Nat didn't know Eskiminzin's Aravaipas were on the rampage, he wouldn't feel the need to be too careful. The Apache in this area had been living peacefully for some time now.

Buckthorn clamped his jaws together, bunching the muscles at their sides. The thing was becoming urgent. He had to get to the party before the Apache did, that was for sure. Though, he thought, it was a damned-fool mission to be on. But, those were his orders, like it or not. Warn people. Guide them into Camp Sweeton, if need be.

He went back down to the overhang again. He looked at the woman. She was still asleep, and in her repose, her face had lost its arrogance. It was white, beautiful, serene, peaceful — if a bit dirty.

Calculatingly now he weighed up the odds. He could risk a small fire. What smoke he would make would be dispersed by the overhang before it reached the horizon of the ravine. And he had wood that made little smoke. Also, right now in the cold of dawn, hot coffee would go down real swell. Make them both feel good . . .

★ ★ ★

It was full light when he awoke Mrs Fairfax with a mug of hot coffee and a plate of beans and fatback.

"The best I have, ma'am," he said.

Her big eyes reached up to look at him. They were swollen with sleep. She appeared subdued and cold. Now, in the light of day he could see her eyes were green; that they were alluring and deep. And intelligent.

She blinked and gave him a long, studied look. He thought he could detect a hint of gratefulness behind her scrutiny.

"Thank you," she said.

She took the coffee and food. She ate slowly and carefully. He noticed though she thoroughly cleaned the plate.

While she did Buckthorn busied himself breaking camp. As he rolled his blanket, he stared at her and indicated to it. He said, more out of curiosity than anything else,

"You didn't use it."

Again the eyes came up, but this time there was a look of distaste about them. "It is dirty," she said.

Buckthorn blinked. Again his anger

flared momentarily. Damn it, the trooper's wife that did his washing had tubbed it for him only two days before he had left Camp Sweeton.

"You're a mighty fussy female," he grunted, tetchily. "It's as clean as it ever will be."

She looked at him in that haughty way she had, rawing his anger even more.

"If that is the case," she said firmly, "it doesn't speak very well of you — or the standards of hygiene you maitain."

He met her sharp stare with fierce eyes, but before he could answer she went on, "And by the way, what is your name? I cannot go on calling you nothing."

Buckthorn found it hard to suppress the rage that now fired through him. He spat his contempt. He could spank the damned female! She had a cutting, supercilious way with her he was rapidly finding hard to stomach.

"Damn it — Linus Buckthorn," he

ground out. He didn't try to stop his jaw jutting aggressively.

As if she hadn't noticed his animosity she got up and stretched with a long, luxurious, lithe movement. After it and with a deep sigh, she attempted to straighten her crumpled, dusty suit.

Watching her it irritated Buckthorn to admit to himself the move had been as graceful as a she-cat stretching on a warm window ledge after she had been sleeping all day in the sun.

Now she had her green gaze on him again, steady and direct, But she seemed strangely hesitant. "Mr Buckthorn," she said. She studied him again. After calculated moments she went on, "I have an urge to satisfy the needs of nature. What do you suggest?" He noticed, as she said it, she coloured slightly.

Buckthorn found he had to think for a second or two to define what she meant. When it came to him, he shuffled, his resentment dying slowly. It must have taken some sinking of dignity on this woman's part to ask that.

"There are some bushes yonder," he said, his voice level. But, even so, he felt the need to add, spitefully, "Ain't maybe what you're used to, but I guess that's all there is right now."

She didn't appear to be put out by what he said. "I have spent many months in the wildernesses of the world," she said loftily. "Sometimes compromises have to be made."

"Such as sharing blankets an' jerky?" Buckthorn rasped. He felt good after he'd said it.

She stared at him again, the green eyes flaring for a moment. "Indeed so, if one feels the need to share them. At the moment, I do not."

She made off for the bushes.

When she returned he had sand-washed the tin plates and cups and frying pan and was packed up, ready and impatiently waiting.

"We'll move, ma'am," he said gruffly.

"I need a wash," she said. "I feel filthy."

"Water's for drinkin', Mrs Fairfax," he grunted.

Without asking he took her round that slim waist and heaved her into the saddle. He climbed up behind her and settled himself on the mare's broad rump.

"I think I know where your husband's camp is," he informed her now. "I hope to God we can get to him before the Apache do."

"What do you mean?" She turned to look at him, slight alarm flashing in her eyes.

"I mean, that smoke he's making is announcing his presence for twenty miles around here," he rasped.

With a grunt Buckthorn sent the roan towards the north-west.

Mrs Fairfax went silent and slumped in front of him. After ten minutes, to his surprise, she leaned back on his deep chest. She seemed tired and listless. Idly, Buckthorn wondered now:

was she beginning to know real fear?

When the terrain permitted, he could see the smoke still reeding into the blue vault. He kept below the ridge tops. It meant a slower progress through the rocky hills, but it also meant a better chance of survival. He had a deep respect for the Apache, and their savvy.

At a small stream, he stopped.

"You can bathe your face if you like, Mrs Fairfax." he offered, his temper long ago cooled. "I have to fill the canteens."

He looked up. The sun was now a brassy ball above them and he had observed for some time sweat running freely down Mrs Fairfax's face and neck. She dabbed it frequently with a small, lace handkerchief. But she was obviously suffering considerable distress. She was also bare-headed, too. Good thing, he thought, her hair was thick, black and shining, like a squaw's.

He slid off the rump of the horse

and helped her down from the saddle. Then he unhitched the canteens for filling. Close by the roan drank deep and long.

Ten minutes later, refreshed, they pressed on again. But this time, above the smoke, and being closer, Buckthorn observed the black-paper shapes of the vultures wheeling in the cobalt vault.

Immediately he saw them, an icy band gripped his stomach. In this country that could only mean one thing: dead, or dying flesh lay below those desert carrion.

Alarmed he looked at the back of Mrs Fairfax's delicate, swan-like neck. From where he sat, she looked a weak, vulnerable woman. God Almighty, he thought, how will she take what lies ahead, if his fears were confirmed?

He felt like avoiding the camp, to spare her pain, but knew he couldn't. Sooner or later she would have to face up to what he expected to find.

★ ★ ★

They came upon the camp around noon. It was beyond a huge upthrust of rock which hid the large stretch of open, relatively flat ground the camp had stood on.

The tents, he assumed the party must have used, were now black ashes, bits of charred canvas clinging to posts, or flopping loosely along in the slow breeze, or caught against scrub.

Buckthorn instantly saw those that hadn't died quickly had been horribly tortured. He swallowed hard. He had to admit to himself, no matter how often he saw these depravations, he was never able to get used to them.

He felt Mrs Fairfax stiffen against him. He heard her gasp. Then her whimpered, stark, disbelieving cry hit the shimmering, furnace air. She started to scream uncontrollably and he was forced to clamp his hand over her mouth again, as he had done last night.

Steely-eyed and hard-faced he climbed down off the roan and brought Mrs

Fairfax down with him.

On a sudden impulse he pulled her to him. For some odd reason he couldn't define, he found he wanted to comfort the hurt he knew was now in her, though wary of her reaction. He had known similar hurts; the death of his mother, and his father's lingering paralysis caused by an Apache attack before he, too, had died.

He found her response surprised him. With suppressed animal noises moaning from her she turned and buried her head into his chest, despite his hand over her mouth. It was as if she thought him something solid and sane in a suddenly insane world. Or, through him, she could hide away from what she had seen.

She clung to him, her body shuddering and trembling violently against him.

Experiencing her response he felt his paternal instincts rise. Unsure about them, he felt clumsy and out of place with them, but somehow knowing instinctively she needed him right now. He patted her raven hair with a gentleness that surprised him.

"I know the pain, ma'am," he said softly. "I know it."

With the cries of the vultures above him, stark and harsh in his alert ears, it seemed an eternity passed while Buckthorn stood there with Mrs Fairfax in his arms, yet he knew it was only moments.

Presently he said quietly, without rancour, "I guess you now know why we have to be quiet, Mrs Fairfax. I guess you fully appreciate the reason for that now."

After seconds she stirred and looked at him. Behind the horror in her eyes — peering over his hand — he saw there was a deep, wounded hurt. A shocked, lost numbness. Then he felt her body slowly relax within his arms, though it still shuddered and quivered like a startled roe deer's. She nodded, dumbly.

He took his hand from her mouth. Her former screams had now sunk down to deep, harrowing whimpers.

She slowly disentangled herself from him, a grateful look in her eyes. But now she walked falteringly to the big, red-haired man lying prone on the ground nearby. She sank to her knees beside him swaying back and forth on her haunches, her hands wringing on nothing only desperate, heart-tearing despair.

His steel-grey gaze following her, Buckthorn could see arrows were sticking out of the man's stomach and chest. Buckthorn could also see Lord Algernon Fairfax had died fighting like a man. That he had sold his life dearly. Bloodstains were all around him. Crimson skids and trails showed where bodies had been dragged away, bad wounded or dead. The guns Fairfax must have used would have been taken, Buckthorn knew. They must now have special medicine.

Grim-faced, Buckthorn wandered through the smouldering camp; the heat and smell of burning timber and canvas, hot and acrid in his nostrils.

He found the bodies of two other men now, behind the charred hulk of a wagon. They were pierced with arrows as well as being gunshot. It looked as though they'd put up a hell of a fight, too.

Behind a clump of scrub he found a woman. The fine silks she had worn were torn and bloody. It was obvious, too, the Apache had had their usual way with her before they had killed her. Her blue eyes stared up at him, the horror of her passing still alive in them.

Then he found the man in the strange dress. He wore a swallow-tailed coat, black pinstripe trousers, red waistcoat, celluloid butterfly collar and black bow tie. He had been disembowelled with what appeared to Buckthorn to be the man's own butcher's knife.

But it was when he found Nathan Foley Buckthorn was almost sick. They had given Nat the full treatment, right down to frying his brains over

68

a slow fire. Damn it, for all his faults, Nathan hadn't deserved that, Buckthorn thought bleakly.

He looked around more fully now. He could see debris everywhere. Evidence of a superior lifestyle. There were shiny candelabra, enamel washbasins and stands to place them in; towels, brushes, soap, bedding, campbeds, fine clothes for both male and female, strewn around. There was fine furniture, too. A long polished table, fancy chairs. It looked as though the goods had been dragged out from the tents and what had been big wagons. Large trunks were scattered about, too, their contents inspected for use, thrown aside if they weren't of any.

Lord Algernon Fairfax, his wife and his friends, Buckthorn reckoned, had lived mighty well. He could now appreciate Mrs Fairfax's haughty demeanour. He hadn't offered much in the way of what she was used to, that was for sure, nor would he be able to. He decided there and then, the quicker he could get her to Camp Sweeton the better for both of them. Their backgrounds were as different as chalk was to cheese.

Meanwhile there was the matter of the bodies.

He hadn't time to dig, that was for sure. The living were more important than the dead right now. Staring round he noticed the flat ground was strewn with rocks, enough to cover the bodies. Sufficient to stop the vultures and coyotes getting at them.

He set to his grim task, after explaining to Mrs Fairfax the necessity of it. He considered it right and proper to assure her, even while she rocked in her grief, men would return for the bodies as soon as it was practical and possible to do so, to ensure a decent Christian interment.

She had looked at him dull-eyed as he gently told her. Throughout, while he went on with the harrowing but necessary business, she remained knelt by the body of her husband until Buckthorn came to drag Lord Fairfax to the burial site.

He could now see her eyes were red-rimmed with weeping. She looked numb, hollowed out. But she did not remonstrate when he caught Lord Fairfax's collar and towed him to the makeshift grave. All she did was listlessly stare at him across the parched ground as he piled up the last stones on the burial cairn.

When he'd finished he moved back to her. She still knelt where her husband had fallen. He saw she was tearless now. Saw that her face was stiff, set, the dust on it smeared with her tears.

"I'm not being much help, am I?" she said; her voice was hollow and harsh.

Though sympathy was heavy within him, Buckthorn found it difficult, nigh impossible, to find any further suitable words of comfort. It just wasn't in his makeup. He'd seen a lot of grief in this bloody land. And had taken most of it stoically.

"We have to be movin', Mrs Fairfax," he said softly. "They say lightning don't strike the same place twice. I ain't ever gone along with that theory, though."

He was surprised when she smiled up at him mirthlessly, almost derisively, from her position on the ground. "You mean our native friends . . . "

Buckthorn nodded. "Yup."

She sighed and got up. Her fine suit was thick with dust. Her raven hair was uncombed and lank, but her bearing was still erect and proud. It gave Buckthorn the impression that her spirit would never be defeated.

He found her green stare was meeting his own steel-grey gaze boldly now, demanding a straight answer.

"Shall we get out of this alive, Mr Buckthorn?" she said.

He shuffled and rubbed his big nose. "I surely hope so. It won't be for the lack of tryin'. I've been in fixes worse than this."

"Then I am in your hands, jerky and all."

Buckthorn looked at her sharply. He looked for sarcasm, or resignation, but there seemed more of a sudden acceptance of what had happened. She seemed to have absorbed her pain, accepted her grief and buried it within her. There also appeared a determination now to go along with him. Further, in her response, he thought he detected, even in these circumstances, a touch of desperate humour.

"It appears so, ma'am," he said.

"But it would not harm to take along a bottle of Algernon's Scotch, would it, Mr Buckthorn?"

Baffled he said, "Scotch?"

"Whisky, bourbon, whatever you call it here."

Taken aback slightly Buckthorn shook his head, surprised and agreeable to the suggestion. But he'd seen no bottles around the camp. However the proposition was attractive, if only the spirit be used to keep the night cold out, for he felt Mrs Fairfax would be using his blanket from now on and he wouldn't.

"Why, no, ma'am, if you can find any."

A frown crossed her fine brow at his remark. She turned and paced over to one of the burnt-out wagons. Eventually she picked up the neck of a broken bottle. She said, "I don't understand. If the fire had got to them, there would be shattered glass all over the place, wouldn't you agree?"

Buckthorn knew he couldn't argue with that, not that there was a need to, even though he had no idea how many bottles she was talking about. He repeated his latter thoughts to her out loud.

"There were three cases of fine French wine," she said, "a supply of Madeira — sherry — oh, several malt whiskies — "

"All good sippin', uh, Mrs Fairfax?" he interrupted.

"All good 'sipping' as you call it," she said.

Now Buckthorn found his brain was working fast. There was the distinct possibility there could be a lot of mighty drunk Apaches near here, knowing their liking for it . . .

Buckthorn looked grimly at her. "We'll move out, ma'am. We got to find you a horse."

She looked at him strangely. "And where can we get one of those?"

Buckthorn allowed himself a grim smile. "The Apaches."

She glared at him. "Are you out of your mind?" she breathed.

"No, ma'am," he countered. Very much in it. There could be a whole heap of very drunk Injuns hereabouts if what you say about your husband's booze is so. They have a fatal likin' for the stuff. In kegs, or bottles, or jugs. It don't matter a damn to them how it comes. They'll drink it by the bucket."

Mrs Fairfax looked curiously at him for moments before her eyes narrowed. He thought he saw a new respect for him come to them. She nodded. "Yes, I gather what you mean," she said. "Are you ready to risk that?"

"Sure, ma'am. If they're drunk, it won't be much risk. It'll be a *bronco* camp, for sure. All men; no women to warn them."

Though she looked a little uncertain she said, "I'm sure you know the ways of the native."

She held herself stiffly now, her features pale, tight and immobile. He noticed her fists were clenched and trembling by her side, knuckle-white. "There is one thing more," she said then.

She turned and knelt at the burial cairn. She prayed silently for fully a minute before she got up.

"I'm ready now, Mr Buckthorn," she said calmly.

"Linus, ma'am," he said. "My name's Linus."

Her sensuous mouth tightened, then a flicker of doubt crossed her brow. "No, Mr Buckthorn, I think our relationship should remain formal for the time being, if you don't mind," she said after moments.

"Formal, ma'am?" Buckthorn hadn't heard that one before.

She looked at him puzzled for a second or two before enlightenment came. "I mean, you will be Mr Buckthorn and I, since you will not use my full title, will be Mrs Fairfax."

After the past recent intimacies Buckthorn felt his anger again. Who the hell were these people? Had they all got starch in their britches? There was more give in a two-inch bar of steel.

He spat and grated harshly, "An' you can go to hell, *Mrs* Fairfax!"

He swung his right arm up. He had found a good quality stetson abandoned amongst the ruins of the camp. He thrust it at her.

"Wear this, *Mrs* Fairfax, before the sun burns a hole right through that starch brain of yours," he rasped harshly.

He turned abruptly to the roan stood close by. "We'll get to ridin'," he growled. "Fact is, I'm getting to thinkin' I'd rather have a gut-low Apache on my ass than a high-nosed female like you!"

4

HIS anger still blazing in him, *Mrs* Fairfax up in front of him, Buckthorn began to search out the trail the Apaches had left.

It wasn't going to be easy, he knew that. But he'd picked up a lot of savvy from the Red Band Apache scouts attached to the army generally. They were asked to wear red headbands to facilitate identification during battle.

But he wanted this high-and-mighty woman off his back. And if he got a horse, he'd be a lot quicker doing it. But as he rode, he relented. The woman had grief, high grief.

The trail led off north-west, towards the snow-capped mountains. He knew the Apaches had strongholds up there. But Buckthorn had a powerful hunch that as soon as the Aravaipas had put distance between them and the killings at Fairfax's camp, the whisky would be flowing.

Unexpectedly he came upon two cairns of rocks, each with a dead Apache planted there. Obviously they wanted to move fast, with no excess baggage. He felt a grim satisfaction in the discovery. Enough to nod at them, nudge *Mrs* Fairfax and point.

"Well, there's one thing, your man and his party can rest easy," he grunted. "I'm sure that's dead proof they took some of the red varmints with them."

She turned round to stare at him with wide, red-rimmed eyes. He could see they were again moist with tears. However, "Algernon would have found no pleasure in taking human life," she informed him curtly. "Even though he was willing to defend himself as a last resort, he would strive for compromise and reason first."

Buckthorn grunted. "The hell he would," he snorted, resenting the haughty return. "Well, I tell you how it happened back there, ma'am.

He would never have had the chance to compromise. On the warpath, Apaches do their talking after they've killed you — usually to boast how they did it. An' as for how *I'd* feel about it, ma'am, it'd sure as hell give me one hell of a boost to know I'd taken two up the trail with me, and an even bigger whoopee to know I'd taken more."

He nodded and spat contentedly at that.

Mrs Fairfax had turned away, had gone quiet, as if she had hardly heard what he had said. She seemed lost in her own thoughts, apparently unimpressed with his boasts.

He growled. Damn it, he thought, what did the woman use for blood? Ice?

Disgruntled he urged the mare on.

★ ★ ★

Twilight hung over them like an orange-gold, silken veil draped across the sky. Buckthorn halted the roan and peered into the huge hollow in the hills they overlooked. Fires pricked the purple distance, looking as though they were glowworms.

"Five bucks it's the Apaches, ma'am," he breathed.

Again she didn't answer, just stared at him. She looked drained, numbed, a little lost. Maybe the woman was taking the death of her husband a lot stronger than he had thought. Maybe it was him that was being unreasonable. The woman couldn't help the way she had been brought up. And she had just had one hell of a shock to her navel.

He looked round. They were in a place suitable enough for an overnight camp and a possible clear run to Fort Sweeton, though mighty doubt crept in about that. First thing he had to do was to get a horse for the woman. The roan was getting mighty tired.

"Settle down here, ma'am, an' keep yourself hidden," he said. "I'm goin' to have to leave you for awhile."

She looked at him sharply, her

green eyes rounding momentarily. He thought he detected apprehension in her stare. But she seemed trained to hide her emotions, except during the most cruel of occasions — like back at her husband's camp.

She said, surprising him, "Please be careful, Mr Buckthorn."

There seemed deep sincerity in her tone. But maybe she meant it would be aces for her own sake he kept his hide intact. He was being damned cynical, he knew, but that was how he felt about her.

"That's my middle name, Mrs Fairfax," he said. "Careful."

He took the saddlebags holding his jerky, biscuits and raisins and put it down beside her, along with two canteens of water.

"Hold on to them, ma'am," he said. "I got to travel as light as I can."

Her eyes studied him in that lofty way she had. Then she said suddenly, sharply, "I am not a fool. This is in case you don't come back, isn't it?"

Though it was, Buckthorn shook his head. "Hell, no, ma'am. It's like I said."

With that he swung up on to the roan. He settled into the familiar saddle, occupied by Mrs Fairfax of late. He stared down at her.

"Stay quiet, ma'am," he advised. "I won't be long. But if I am, walk west till I catch up with you."

He pointed the way.

Her fine chin came up. She looked at him with those deep, green eyes. "I understand, Mr Buckthorn," she said. "Quite clearly."

He nodded. For all her damned faults, the woman had guts to spare. He had to give her that.

His jaw set in a grim line he turned towards the fires now pricking the purple twilight maybe two miles ahead.

"I may be an hour or two," he said.

★ ★ ★

It was like he thought it would be. They were raising merry joy down here. And at the moment they must feel it was reasonably safe to do so, too, he reckoned. They had booty and food, were well into the foothills — almost into the mountains — and had a big head start.

Hell. Why shouldn't they let their hair down? Buckthorn studied. They had a lot to celebrate. And a lot to forget, too. Like the deaths of their wives and children.

Buckthorn blinked in the full dark at that thought. Well, right now, he wasn't the least bit concerned about that. They had wreaked their revenge. Now it was all square again in his book. And it had always been kill or be killed, with no qualms.

He dismounted. The camp he looked down on was a stop-over, he knew. No wickiups. Nothing. Just a place to drink and forget for a few hours before the army took them on and a fighting retreat began. Counting them as best he could as they danced and drank and collapsed he tallied twenty-two braves down there, highlighted by the fires.

Now Buckthorn could see their horses were rope-corralled north. He would have to work his way right round the camp to reach them.

He licked his dry lips and raised his thin brows. Well, there was only one thing to do, and that was to get to it.

He remounted and eased, with infinite caution, around the camp. Already some of the Apaches were dropping, bottle in hand and going limp, plunged, no doubt, into an alcohol-induced sleep. Others were singing in high-pitched voices, still dancing round the fires.

As he approached the remuda, Buckthorn increasingly became more alert. They could, just possibly, have posted guards. But, Buckthorn also knew, the Apache could be very naive on occasion. Very confident. Very relaxed. This seemed to be one of them.

The remuda was unattended.

As well as the small, wiry mustangs the Apache rode, sometimes cruelly and sometimes to death before they ate them, Buckthorn could see eight very good quarter horses amongst them. Fairfax's string . . . ?

The songs from the camp were becoming increasingly slurred as the fine wines and good whiskies were consumed with increasing zest. The brews must, sure as hell, beat tizwin, Buckthorn decided grudgingly. Damn it, it could have been him partaking instead of the red devils, if the time had been right.

It was then he saw the brave sleeping close to the remuda, his head nestled into the bow of a fine saddle. He was sprawled out, bottle in hand, a smile on his flat face.

Buckthorn narrowed his gaze. The decision came swiftly. He had to have that saddle. He wasn't sure Mrs Fairfax could ride bareback. That aside, though; it was a fine piece of leather, anyway. Wasted on Apaches.

Now he waited, grim-faced, for the drink to take full effect. Slowly the camp became increasingly less rumbustious and a near half-moon lifted above the eastern horizon.

Buckthorn tied up the roan in the shelter of a clutch of rocks some hundred yards from the remuda, gave it a nosebag of oats. The last of his stock.

He found his body tensing up now, his senses, already alert, keening up to a new pitch of awareness. It had to be now or never, he decided. He moved forward, his eyes narrow and keen.

Close now, looking at the horses, he selected a fine bay.

When he got in amongst them they began to hustle around restlessly and noisily.

Pausing, breath held, Buckthorn blinked and stared around him.

His barometer was the brave sleeping close by, his head on the saddle. If he didn't move, he figured there was a fair chance the others wouldn't. He froze and watched the brave. Not a flicker of life.

Relieved Buckthorn caught the bay by the mane, took it through the restless mustangs. He led it out of the remuda, leaving the confining rope he had undone, trailing, inviting the rest of the horses to stray.

He led the bay to where his roan was and put his lariat round its neck and secured it to some mesquite.

With his right hand he wiped away the thin sheen of sweat on his broad brow. Though cooling, the night was still close. He set his jaw. Now for the saddle . . .

He drew his long, slim skinning knife. Maybe he would have to use it, maybe not. He reckoned the brave was too dead drunk to know anything — even if he was stomped on by a horse.

He crouched and moved forward, his powerful legs rippling under his doeskin trousers.

As he approached, Buckthorn could see the Indian was still in a drunken stupor. A smile was on his flat, dark-brown face and he appeared completely comatose. Buckthorn thought, man, I could slit your throat and send you up to that place in the sky and you'd still be smiling, never knowing what put you up on that cloud.

He buried his grim thoughts. The Indian could live if he didn't wake up, he decided. Buckthorn had never been a man for killing in cold blood. Then he thought of the children at Alvaro Galvo's casa and wished he didn't have such scruples.

Now, this close up, he could see the saddle was obviously an expensive one. One of Fairfax's saddles . . . ?

But it was of no matter at the moment. What mattered was getting it from under the head of the smiling Indian and on to the back of the bay.

Buckthorn tucked his knife into his belt. With his left hand he eased the Aravaipa's head up and with his right hand slowly eased away the saddle. With the same care, he lowered the head to the ground.

The Apache moved restlessly when he did that. Swiftly, Buckthorn pulled the knife. He brought the blade to within a fraction of the brave's throat. For a brief moment Buckthorn wished the red devil would open his eyes.

Now the brave broke wind, wriggled sloppily, smiled and turned on to his right side and started to breathe deeply again.

Buckthorn slowly relaxed; looked about him. The camp was still, the fires dying. They were damned sure of themselves, he thought, with a tinge of resentful anger. If only he had a troop of cavalry with him. It would have been all over by now for this bunch of marauding killers, that was for sure. They'd be just a bunch of statistics in the offices at headquarters.

Buckthorn shrugged. What the hell. He hadn't a troop of cavalry. He'd nothing, only his own cussedness.

He crept into the night again, to where he had left the horses.

Soon he had the saddle on the back of the bay. He took the nosebag off the roan, stowed it and mounted. Now for the Indian horses, he thought. The logical thing was to scatter them all over the foothills. And once he had decided upon it, he didn't think twice about it.

Leading the bay, he moved out. Within a couple of minutes he was amongst the Indian mounts. Immediately he began to flail at them with the other end of his lariat he had the bay tied to. Already some of the mustangs had strayed out through the gap he had left in the rope, foraging for feed.

Now the ponies and horses began to snort and whistle and run. He beat it up after them; lashing out where he could until all the horses were truly on their way to freedom.

They ran into the night, shrilling their joy.

Now he turned and looked back at

the camp. In the moonlight, he could see men staggering drunkenly around, their angry shouts clear in the still night.

He whooped and put the roan into a run for the place where he had left Mrs Fairfax. But he had no doubts. It was a different game now — now the Apache knew he was around . . . And he knew they had the stamina to outstay a horse over a period of time. And they were like goats in the mountains on foot, their legs as strong as steel. He wasn't out of the woods yet. If anything, he decided, he was deeper in them.

They knew now.

5

BACK at the place where he had left Mrs Fairfax, Buckthorn dismounted tiredly. He found she had settled herself in a concealing niche in the rocks. She was chewing on some jerky.

"We have to be leaving, ma'am," he said, without preliminaries.

She looked at him in that direct, bold sort of way she had. "I expected you not to return," she said, slight surprise in her voice. "After all, what am I to you, other than a nuisance?"

Buckthorn met her stare. It was the way she said it. As though she didn't give a damn; that she would make out. She was a spunky lady, he had to give her that. And he knew a few men who would have done just what she assumed he might do.

"You don't seem to appreciate how

things work out here, ma'am," he said. "As a scout for the army forces here, I have been given a job to do. Warn people about the Apache, bring them into Camp Sweeton as best I can if they request it. I use my own discretion there. Fact is though, most folks out here are able to take care of themselves."

Her face altered in the moonlight, became haughty. "Meaning I am not?"

Now occupied with his lariat, Buckthorn looked at her sidewise; met her bold stare. "Speakin' blunt. Yes."

"I have more experience than you think," she said, challenge and pride in her voice.

"Then there ain't nothin' to stop us parting trail now if you so wish it, is there, Mrs Fairfax?" he commented dryly. He felt happy to call her weak bluff.

As if put out by the remark she got up and started pacing about, her arms wrapped around her, as if hugging herself. "I'm grateful for your expertise and — and — your company, rough though it is, Mr Buckthorn. But I don't want you to think I'm helpless."

Buckthorn spat. "I've never thought that, ma'am," he said untruthfully.

"You have given me that impression repeatedly."

"I have, ma'am?" he said.

"Yes," she said.

Damn the woman, he thought irritably. Why did she have to think she needed to defend herself all the time? Why didn't she admit, if only to herself, she was next to useless out here and shut up? There were much more pressing matters to deal with. Why didn't she grieve, instead of holding it inside her? He could understand that and make allowances.

With a growl Buckthorn busied himself making a makeshift bridle for his own roan out of a length of his lariat. He would put his mount's bridle on the bay. He was not sure of Mrs Fairfax's horsemanship and there wasn't time to test it.

Buckthorn fitted the rope bridle to his mare. At first she snorted and chucked her head a bit, but he coaxed her to accept it.

Now he met Mrs Fairfax's stare with narrow eyes. She was a woman of contradictions. High-and-mighty one minute, seeking guarded assurance the next. But for the most part, as far as he was concerned, she was a pain in the butt.

"Your horse is ready, Mrs Fairfax," he said.

She looked at the bay, for the first time. Seeing it, she gasped. "Oh, my God," she breathed. "That is my husband's horse — Marcus." Her eyes rounded, stared at him, hurt clear in them. "How could you?"

Buckthorn stiffened, his anger rising. "Damn it, ma'am," he growled. "How in Hades was I to know?"

But he noticed she had gone very pale; that her face was disturbed, sad and shiny in the moonlight. It was obvious she was now struggling with some deep, hurting emotion.

After moments she straightened her back and held her head up. Her hands were clenched into white-knuckled fists, her arms held tightly to her sides.

She whispered then, "I'm being a fool. Accept my apologies. My reaction was unforgivable."

He spat, his irritation subsiding. The woman was like a burr under a saddle sometimes. But it was now becoming obvious she had felt a lot for her man.

"Think nothin' of it, ma'am," he said. "But to get back to the matters to hand, we should be ridin'."

She took a deep breath, compressed her lips. "Yes, of course. I am being a very silly woman."

Not wanting to comment on that, Buckthorn said, "I'll help you into the saddle, Mrs Fairfax."

She hesitated a moment and glanced at him, her usual aplomb now seemingly fully gathered again. "I usually ride side-saddle," she now complained a little petulantly.

Buckthorn tightened his lips, roping down his anger. He spat. "Well, ma'am, you're just goin' to have to forgo that little pleasure for a while, ain't you," he fired back.

He grabbed her by that slim waist of hers again. He could not feel any whalebone underneath supporting it which surprised him. He lifted her up into the saddle. She settled into it and stared straight ahead, her face set and angular.

Now in his own saddle and using the stars to guide him towards Camp Sweeton, Buckthorn urged his roan into the night asking Mrs Fairfax to pull the bay in behind him. He was secretly pleased to notice she looked at ease in the saddle.

He knew this part of the foothills was smoother, less rocky; that they had a rolling, breast-like shape. Grass, though brown, was more abundant and stunted trees became more plentiful.

As he rode Buckthorn gnawed on some jerky, offered some to Mrs

Fairfax. She refused it.

By his reckoning, another day and a half they would be into Camp Sweeten. He sighed inwardly. He had the feeling it was going to be one of the more trying periods of his life, Apaches aside, unless the female improved mighty fast.

★ ★ ★

At dawn Buckthorn guided the woman into the narrow, verdant ravine he had been heading for. He knew it was sheltered and hidden and that a stream bubbled through it.

"Climb down, Mrs Fairfax," he invited. "Rest easy."

He put the horses on hobbles and secured them to aspens on long ropes. He left them to graze. He moved a short way upstream now and hooked two fine fish in the pool he knew was up there.

When he came back he found Mrs Fairfax washing her head and hair by the stream. Her graceful beauty stirred him momentarily. But she was always preening, he thought. Damn it, she could have been looking for kindling for the fire. That was more important at the moment. Then again, she wouldn't know the kind that burned with the least smoke. And, putting two and three together, five up she'd never had to do a damned thing for herself in her life if he read her right.

He found wood, built a fire and boiled coffee. He gutted and skewered the fish on green sticks and baked them over the flames. When they were nicely cooked he put one of the fish on a plate along with his only fork and offered it to her.

He observed she had found a comb from somewhere and was teasing out her raven locks. In a strange way her features, made wax-like with fatigue and grief, had taken on a new, elegant beauty.

She smelt the fish first, then attacked it hungrily. It seemed no time at all she had eaten it but for the bones. She even smiled at him as he sat, gnawing at his own fish between his fingers.

"I must say that was most pleasant," she said.

Buckthorn looked at her and grinned for the first time in many hours. Strange how food relaxed a man, he thought. And a woman too, it seems . . .

"Ain't nothing finer," he said. "Straight out of the stream, over the fire and on to the plate."

"Yes," she agreed. "Indeed. So simple."

Now she sighed and gazed at him with those big, green eyes.

"Well, what now, Mr Buckthorn?"

"I figure we'll maybe sleep a while, ma'am. Rest the horses. Move on late afternoon. Travel through the night."

"And what about the savages?"

"They can see less at night, are reluctant to attack then anyway, and the day's heat is draining to travel through."

"But shouldn't we be pressing on to safety?"

"Yes, ma'am, at the right time." He blinked at her. "You find a cosy niche, Mrs Fairfax. We both need rest."

Though the woman seemed unsure she said, "Well, I am completely in your hands, Mr Buckthorn."

Buckthorn felt a certain contentment at that. That was about the first sensible thing the female had come out with since first meeting up with her.

"That's the size of it," he said.

While he dowsed the fire and tidied camp, Mrs Fairfax carried on combing her hair, sat on a rock by the stream. Finally he felt he had to come out with that other thing that had been sticking in his craw for some time.

"Ma'am, it's customary for everybody to lend a hand in camp."

Her relaxed face tightened. She stared at him haughtily. "I have never done a menial task in my life. How dare you suggest it?"

Buckthorn felt his anger rising against

the woman again, against that sharp tongue of hers and her manner. He wasn't sure what menial meant, but he had a feeling it wasn't polite. Damn it, it was like striking a flint saying some things to this woman. The sparks flew straightaway. And she had a downright clear habit of looking down on a man.

"Ma'am, I've a daring nature," he growled meanly. "And I don't give a hoot in hell what you did before we met up. But I'm telling you now, from now on you're going to pull your weight around here."

He threw the tin coffee cups, pot and plate they had used for breakfast at her feet. "Here's where you start. Clean those."

She stood up and stared at him, her green eyes flashing. She had a slim, erect figure. Still as proud as the Arab mare he had first likened her with, he thought. He guessed her age to be around thirty years.

Her chin lifted. "Mr Buck — "

He cut in on her with a harsh voice. "The damned pots, ma'am!" he said, warning in his tone.

She glared, real fire in her eyes now. "Clean pots?" she returned contemptuously. "I shall do no such thing!"

Buckthorn broke. He'd had enough of this arrogant bitch. With one swift, lithe movement he pulled her over his knee and spanked her soundly while she squirmed and raged.

He let her go. She was upright and staring at him immediately. If her eyes had held fire before, he observed, they now sparkled with furious green flames. "You coarse, uncouth wretch I — I — "

Her towering anger extinguished her voice.

Livid she aimed a kick at him which he evaded easily. She finished up on her bustle, glaring up at him. Again she was on her feet with that lithe movement of hers, her long skirt apparently not a hindrance.

To relieve her anger now she swung round and kicked the crocks across the grass. "That's what I think of you, sir, and your unspeakable pots!"

Rubbing her rear she stomped off and attempted to sit down in the shade of an aspen. Finally, as if finding it painful, she lay down on her right side. Buckthorn could hear her muttering darkly to herself.

His frustration and resentment satisfied, Buckthorn simmered down. Hell, he'd never met a more haughty and irritable female. But he felt a whole lot better for spanking her. Damn it, if ever a woman needed it, she did.

But as he settled down to sleep he regretted the necessity. Damn it, the woman still had grief. He ought not have done that . . .

★ ★ ★

It was already gathering purple shadows in the ravine. The sun had left the bottom of it some time ago, though it was still blue and light overhead.

Appreciating the cooler air Buckthorn woke Mrs Fairfax with coffee and beans. She looked surprised and a little puzzled, as if it was totally unexpected. She didn't speak, just took the food.

Buckthorn, grateful for her silence, happily ate.

When Buckthorn had finished his meal, he went to gather the woman's plate and cup. She held up a delicate, slim hand. He looked up sharply. He met her green, quick gaze.

"Leave them to me, Mr Buckthorn," she said then.

She hesitated before she spoke again. It seemed to Buckthorn it was hurting her to say the next words but that she felt she had to say them. "You were perhaps right this morning," she offered grudgingly. "In an extreme situation like this one must forget one's status, though I resent most strongly the way you expressed your disapproval."

Mildly surprised she had climbed down, Buckthorn grunted. "You do, huh? Well I'm glad we're beginning to understand each other."

With a disgruntled growl he left the woman to go into the bushes to meet nature's requirements.

Five minutes later, coming back and nearing the camp area, though it was still screened by bushes, he stiffened. Through a gap in the growth he could see the Apache was standing staring at the woman. Mrs Fairfax, her lips tight, her eyes staring boldly straight at the brave, was standing back by the stream. The frying pan was held high over her head.

"Don't you dare come near me!" she was threatening.

The Apache looked around him now, warily, as if he was mildly startled by finding a solitary white woman in the middle of nowhere. He looked highly suspicious about it, too. Even so he started grinning and leering at her. From where he was Buckthorn could read exactly what was in the red devil's mind.

The brave glanced at the two horses now. Buckthorn could see he'd weighed the situation up pretty quick.

With swift, agile strides the buck went straight for Mrs Fairfax, chittering a bird call as he went. And to Buckthorn that meant another Apache, maybe more.

Damn it!

Now the buck was grabbing for Mrs Fairfax, who was backing across the stream.

"Keep away, you heathen," she warned shrilly. She lifted the frying pan higher.

Buckthorn loosened his frame and began to move swiftly through the bushes, skinning knife drawn and ready. He had to keep it quiet, if he could.

He could see Mrs Fairfax's face was now white and determined. She continued to step back. Now Buckthorn appreciated she had seen him and his heart skipped a beat. She could give the whole damned move away if she showed any sign she had. Destroy his surprise.

But she didn't. She seemed to realize what was necessary. She just kept backing away slowly, pan aloft, her face not altering.

Buckthorn watched as the Apache made to grab her. He could hear the brave's guttural mouthings. He was small. He looked swift. Sinewy. Deadly. But as he lunged for her the woman brought the frying pan down on his head. Buckthorn could hear the ring of the cast iron as it hit his skull.

The buck staggered away with a yell before he recovered. Now he moved angrily towards Mrs Fairfax, blood running down the side of his face. His eyes were slitted and evil. Death dwelled in them.

Death for the woman.

Buckthorn could see amazement on Mrs Fairfax's face. The buck had not fallen to the ground unconscious. She stared at him open-mouthed, the pan hung loosely at her side as he came towards her.

Buckthorn was through the brush now and moving across the open ground. He drove his long-bladed knife up into the heart from behind, his hand around the buck's mouth to stifle his yell.

He could feel the warm blood running on to his hand before he snatched the blade out.

Buckthorn could see Mrs Fairfax's face was now round-eyed and shocked. Her hand was trembling to her mouth to stifle her gasp. It appeared to be her first encounter with sudden, human death.

Buckthorn dropped the brave and took her hand with his bloody paw and towed her with him.

He hissed, "We gotta move, ma'am. Follow me an' say nothin'."

The chitter of the bird call came back in answer to the now dead brave's call. As best he could, Buckthorn mimicked it as he moved. It would maybe reassure who else was out there and give him some time to gather himself, develop strategy.

His mind was now working hard. All their gear was in camp. Saddles, food, everything. He glanced across at the horses. They knew something wasn't right. They were moving restlessly at their tethers. He had to defend them, come what.

He drew his Remington New Army. He would maybe have to use it, despite the noise. He didn't know what else he was up against. And he cursed the fact his Winchester was in its saddleboot, leant against a tree.

He sank down in a cluster of rocks and listened. Mrs Fairfax was trembling beside him, even though she outwardly appeared calm.

The bird call came again. This time Buckthorn didn't answer, but located the position it had come from . . . off to his left. Seemed him/they — he didn't know which — were working round to the horses.

His whole body was alert now, his senses honed to acute awareness. He could hear his heartbeats throbbing in his ears. His whole body pulsated, too. He thought it was like the tolling bell of hell ringing inside him. And he felt sure the Apache could hear it and Mrs Fairf-

The buck hit without warning from behind. The force of his feet into his back sent Buckthorn's breath gusting out of him, his gun jolting out of his hand with the impact. Now the brave was upon him. Buckthorn could smell the gamey smell of the Indian's flesh pressed against his.

With desperate eyes Buckthorn saw the flash of the brave's blade above him in the gathering evening light.

Frantically he caught the buck's knife arm as it came sweeping down. He clamped it in his iron grip. The buck's breath was foul against his face, reeking of alcohol. Damn it, how had they got here so fast . . . ?

But astounded by it, Buckthorn could

now see Mrs Fairfax was on the Apache's back, her fingernails clawing at the buck's face. With an alarmed yell the Apache arched up, throwing the woman off him, sending her rolling into the brush.

Buckthorn, glad of the momentary distraction, hung on and clamped his right hand around the buck's throat and squeezed. He gripped grimly with his other hand, still holding the Apache's knife arm. He managed to roll on top of the brave.

The Apache threshed now and writhed under him, striving to draw life's air into his lungs. And all the time the warrior was straining mightily under Buckthorn, trying to get his knife into him before it was too late.

Buckthorn held on, fighting the Apache with all the power he could summon to his corded, whiptight arm muscles.

Gradually he felt the buck's threshings become less violent. Buckthorn squeezed tighter until he realized the brave had finally gone still and silent under him.

It seemed to Buckthorn he had been hanging on for hours. He daren't let go, his whole strength bunched and locked into this death struggle.

"He's dead, Mr Buckthorn."

The voice shocked him, pulling him out of the red fight-fury he was in. It was off to his right. Close. It was calm and measured. He realized it was Mrs Fairfax.

Buckthorn came out of the crimson mist he was staring through. He was on his hands and knees over the Apache's iron-hard, small, muscular body. He looked down into dead, beady, black eyes. They stared up at him from a swarthy, bloated, fierce, arrogant face bloated by strangulation.

He found his thoughts were gathering themselves quickly, desperately. Had the band split up to search for the horses? he wondered. Were there just two of them? Had they come upon himself and Mrs Fairfax by chance? He knew this ravine was well-hidden.

It seemed likely, he concluded. Had there been more, he and Mrs Fairfax would have been dead now, or captured and lined up for some fearful torture ritual.

6

BUCKTHORN got slowly to his feet and looked around him for his Remington New Army pistol.

He picked it up and examined it. It appeared to be OK. But he'd need to check the loads more closely later.

To his right Mrs Fairfax said, shakily, "You saved my life, Mr Buckthorn."

Buckthorn stared at her. He was still hyped after the death fight. The adrenalin was still active.

"You think what you want to, ma'am," he grunted, surprised by the hint of admiration in her voice. "Meantime, we'll break camp and get to riding. I've a feeling this country is about to become very lively with hungover Apaches."

She seemed slightly deflated he had dismissed her compliment so readily.

Truth was, Buckthorn admitted to himself grudgingly, in the first instance he maybe had been defending the lady, but in the second, hell, it had been his hide on the line. If anything, by jumping on the buck's back, she had maybe saved his! But, by God, he couldn't tell her that. There would be no knowing what that would lead to.

He began gathering the camp equipment. Without prompting, Mrs Fairfax started to saddle the bay and slip on the bridle. He was gratified to see she did it expertly.

Now she doused the fire with water from the stream.

Within minutes they were trailing up the long slope out of the ravine. But just below its rim, Buckthorn eased the roan to a stop. He signalled the woman to do the same. He dismounted and bellied to the rimrock and used his binoculars to survey the country beyond. Already it was going purple-dark in the hollows, the last of the sun was gashing red-yellow light across it before that, too, went.

He could see nothing: only rolling, tree-studded mauve hills swelling west in restless, choppy waves. But that was what he expected to find. Even though they were maybe out there looking for their horses, the Apache would still move with consummate stealth.

As satisfied as he could be their route was reasonably clear he remounted and moved quickly over the skyline and down the other side of the slope into the thinly-wooded narrow valley below, the woman following. They had a night of cautious riding ahead of them. Maybe the Apache was reluctant to attack at night, he mused, believing their souls could lose their way in the dark. But it had been known on moonlit nights. He set his senses on full alert.

★ ★ ★

By his timepiece, taken out of a small inner pocket of his buckskin coat,

Buckthorn found it was five o'clock in the morning. He was bone-tired, drained after the excitement of the fight in the ravine and the long night ride.

He turned in the saddle and stared for moments at the grey, pale dawn streaking the eastern horizon behind him. Too, ranging in his stare now, he could see the woman was drawn-faced and slumped in the saddle, her green eyes dull as they met his gaze from under the broad brim of her hat.

Now looking across at the creek running to his left Buckthorn could see the homestead down there had been gutted. He knew it was Luke Marsden's place. He had given Luke ample warning to pull out before he had rode on to Alvaro Galvo's *casa*.

He stared at the smouldering ruin of the homestead. A warmth of anger rippled through his stomach. Even though it was empty, it hadn't stepped the Apache firing the place. It would maybe take another six months to rebuild. Whether Marsden had taken any livestock with him, Buckthorn could only speculate about. He hadn't stayed to watch them leave, having to warn people further on.

Luke had a big family, too. There was Mary, his wife; their five children: Sarah, Billy, the twins Mark and Sally, the babe, three-year-old Lucy. And he had observed before he left, Mary was carrying again.

Buckthorn sniffed now, stared at the burnt-out hulk. He recalled Luke Marsden had railed against going.

Buckthorn didn't usually advise but this time he had felt he'd had to. He had said, "Hell, Luke, you got young childer' to consider."

"We gotta stay put sometime," Marsden had countered stubbornly.

"Maybe on your own, if you've a mind to," Buckthorn had conceded. "That's your own decision. But when there's a wife and kids . . ."

Marsden had spat, still reluctant. "You think it as bad as that?"

"Could be."

"Only could be?"

"Hell, you know the Apache, Luke. I don't have to paint a picture."

Buckthorn recalled Marsden had nodded. "Well, I'm grateful for your concern, Linus, and you comin' to warn me, but do you think they'll come this far west? Surely they'll head north for the mountains . . . ?"

Feeling the chill dawn Buckthorn spat now, still staring at the burnt-out homestead.

. . . He had emphasized to Marsden: "They're bound to raid for vittles an' horses first. It ain't worth riskin', Luke. Take them in."

Marsden had eyed him with a pale, washed-out stare. "I'll think hard on it, Linus. "You have my word on that."

Buckthorn remembered now he'd been a mite angry with the response. It had made him feel he was wasting his time risking his own hide coming out here to warn them.

"Damn it, do it, Luke," he had grumbled, "them Aravaipas'll sure as hell be mighty riled up."

Luke hadn't taken offence. Instead he'd smiled. "Light and eat, Linus," he had invited, not giving him a positive answer.

Buckthorn felt the warm angry heat he had felt then, now. He had done his job. After that it had been down to Luke.

He had answered more calmly, "Thanks for the offer, Luke, but I ain't time. Gotta be travellin'. If you've sense, you'll be doin' the same," he had added firmly.

* * *

Eyes still narrow Buckthorn let the roan sidle down the slope to the charred homestead.

Mrs Fairfax rode silently behind him.

Buckthorn couldn't see any livestock. Then he saw Luke, strapped to the corral rails . . .

Almost immediately he heard Mrs Fairfax retching behind him. "Oh, my

God," she gasped after moments. "Oh, my God . . . "

Buckthorn could see the coyotes had been at Luke, too, what was left of him. Damn him, Buckthorn's thoughts raged with a sudden gut-flare of anger. He could've thought of the kids.

Then they found the other members of the family . . .

Mrs Fairfax kept moaning by his side and saying, "Dear God, dear God. Oh, my God."

Buckthorn found himself saying now, more to relieve his own sense of revulsion and anger than get at the woman, "You think your ambassador would've saved you an' your lord now, Mrs Fairfax?"

She glared at him across the bare stretch of ground between them with round, horror-filled eyes. "That is most unfair. Terribly unfair."

It was then Buckthorn heard the whimper. It was coming from behind the stone chimney, pointing like an accusing finger to the sky from the cold ashes around it.

Alerted he got off the roan with a lithe, cautious movement. He moved towards the noise. As he rounded the blackened, heat-splintered chimney he saw little three-year-old Lucy. She was rocking back and forth, hugging a rag. doll. Her small round face beneath her tousled curly locks was dirty and tear-stained.

Buckthorn swamped his utter astonishment. How she had survived the attack only God knew. That she had lived until now was an even greater miracle.

He bent down beside her.

"Lucy." He touched her lightly on the shoulder. It was covered by her torn, filthy dress.

Feeling him touch her she jumped. Now her big brown eyes stared up at him. She blinked when she saw him. "Mr Linus, where's Mommy?"

With a terrible anger simmering deep within him, Buckthorn lifted the mite gently and pressed her to his chest.

"Why, honey, I guess she may have gone to the river."

He couldn't think of anything else.

"I'm thirsty," Lucy whimpered in his ear. "I'm hungry."

Lucy started to sob again.

Buckthorn felt clumsy. He'd had few dealings with children. "Sure, honey," he said softly. "I got some raisins, all the way from Californy. How's that?"

He was aware now that Mrs Fairfax was beside him.

"Shall I take her, Mr Buckthorn?" she said as if she had sensed his awkwardness. "I have two children of my own, now at boarding-school. Perhaps some water and a few raisins, as you say."

Though he knew nothing of boarding-schools Buckthorn nodded thankfully and passed Lucy to the woman. She took the child gently, started to coo to her, murmur soothing words.

Buckthorn went to his saddlebags. He poured a cup of water and took the last handful of raisins.

The child drank thirstily, coughing because she gulped too quickly.

"Easy, honey, easy," Buckthorn said softly. "Slowly. Slowly."

Now he offered the raisins to her one by one. They disappeared with equal alacrity.

Now the sun's rays burst across the creek and smacked into the hills west, splashing warm yellow light all over them. It was out of place, such beauty; not part of this grim scene at all, Buckthorn thought.

He continued to give water sips and raisins until Lucy, with sobs that came from somewhere deep inside her slowly relaxed. Finally she fell asleep curled in Mrs Fairfax's arms.

It was only then the woman looked up at him.

"What are we to do, Mr Buckthorn?" she pleaded, her own fatigue evident on her white face. "In this awful country, what are we to do now?"

"Go on, ma'am," he said, "until we

get to Camp Sweeton."

"What about the dead?"

Buckthorn set his lips into a grim line. Had he been on his own, well, he might have taken the chance and buried them. He stared at Mrs Fairfax and Lucy. But the living came first.

"The coyotes have already started their work," he said quietly. "I guess we'll have to leave it at that."

The green eyes flashed up at him for a moment. "But . . . " Mrs Fairfax dropped her gaze. She looked at the child in her arms and brushed away a strand of hair that was stuck to the infant's damp brow.

"You are right, of course," she said hollowly.

"We have to move from here, ma'am," he said now. "Too open. I got a hideout figured for the day. We'll move on to that."

He took the child off her. Lucy didn't even move, just made a shuddering whimper. But, Buckthorn noticed, slumber gave a serene peace to her face. Now, one-handed, Buckthorn helped Mrs Fairfax into the saddle.

She looked down at him now, her green gaze steady. "I'll take the child," she said, more like an order.

Buckthorn studied her with steel-grey eyes. It really didn't need thinking about. He nodded and passed up the sleeping Lucy. In the saddle himself he turned the roan and headed west alongside the creek before cutting back into the hills.

There he made camp again; again risked a small fire and cooked breakfast. The fatback was about finished, so were the beans. The next meal would have to come from the land, or the stream.

Lucy awoke asking for her momma. But she ate the cut up fatback and mashed beans; gulped watered-down coffee. It was obvious she was starved.

Buckthorn was surprised and pleased with the way Mrs Fairfax coaxed and calmed Lucy, cleaned her gently in the stream, tended to her other needs.

Wrapped in Buckthorn's blanket while Mrs Fairfax washed her dress, the child shivered, though the morning was warming up. She was obviously weak from hunger and fatigue. But she clung to Mrs Fairfax's riding skirt with a fierce, nervous tenacity, her big brown eyes round and bewildered.

Buckthorn left them both asleep, huddled together under the ledge of rock he had made camp. He had some hunting to do.

He soon found a rabbit run and took out his wire hang, a permanent part of his equipment.

He left it set to fish. Now he lay under the bushes hanging over the pool by the stream, his eyes, when not on the rock-pool, constantly searching the rimrock around him.

He hooked four fine fish in quick time. Then he heard the rock bouncing and rattling down from the rocky, broken top of the shallow ravine.

Gut-taut, and with infinite care, he wrapped fingers round his Winchester beside him. He buried into the grass beneath the bushes and looked up.

Four braves atop wiry ponies. He recognized one straightaway. Broken Nose, an Aravaipa sub-chief. Bad medicine, any which way you looked at it.

The group were paused, their narrow, coal-black, beady eyes searching the bottom of the shallow ravine. They lingered for fully a minute before disappearing over the horizon, heading north-west.

He breathed out.

Well, they appeared to be searching. Maybe they had found the bucks he had killed and were looking for hides to peel in revenge . . .

He went back to the hang he had set. A plump doe was hung in it. He gutted it. He moved back down to the camp. The two he had left were still asleep under the ledge.

Broken Nose had headed north-west, taking him away from them. Buckthorn looked around the camp once more.

When he was satisfied they were hidden as well as it was possible to be he lay down.

Within moments he was asleep. But it was a troubled sleep.

7

THE rattle and scrape of hooves on rock woke Buckthorn.

A swift glance at the sun told him it was getting near to sunset, maybe an hour or so away. Now his gaze found the woman and Lucy. They were still asleep under the ledge.

He rose with a lithe, cat-like grace from the niche he had selected for himself in the rocks. He saw the swirl of dust now, rising above the ravine edge.

His gut tightened.

Apaches?

Taking his Winchester he snaked up through the bushes and rocks to the rimrock. He peered over with cautious eyes. The trooper rode twenty yards below the rim. Obviously a flanker. Buckthorn recognized him to be trooper Albert Frame.

Belief flooded through Buckthorn. Now he could see, maybe a quarter of a mile away, a strung-out column of about twenty soldiers: dusty, sat deep in their saddles. He could also see the burly figure of Lieutenant Harvey Swale at their head, Sergeant Walter Bushy beside him.

It was clearly a column from Camp Sweeton.

Buckthorn popped up above the rim. "Howdy, Albert."

Frame swung round, his Springfield rifle coming up to his shoulder. As he did so he threw a sharp cry,

"Yo . . . the column!"

"Hold on," Buckthorn called, seeing the finger white on the trigger of Frame's rifle. "It's me — Linus Buckthorn."

Frame lowered the Springfield and stared, his long lean face taut. "Hell, you ought to be easy how you spring up on a man," he breathed. "And, hell, you've been feared dead."

Buckthorn grinned back. "They

oughta know me better than that."

The file of cavalrymen had stopped now and Lieutenant Harvey Swale was galloping up towards them.

Buckthorn watched his progress. He was a young, solid man with a square, strong face and bushy sideburns. His eyes were stone-grey and hard. They'd been on a few patrols together. Buckthorn knew him to be a little stiff, but open to argument.

"Linus," Swale said. "What have you got to report?"

Buckthorn blinked. That was Swale. Git right down to it. No glad to see you. Nothing like that. A military man to his toenails, our Lieutenant Swale.

Buckthorn gave him the full story.

"By God," Swale burst out. Buckthorn watched the lieutenant's jaw drop as he said it. "You have Lady Amanda Fairfax?"

"That's the handle she gave me," he said. "Some kind of fine folk from back East, I guess. You know about her?"

No asking about little Lucy Marsden, Buckthorn thought.

Swale glared, his face stiffening. "Her husband is Lord Fairfax, an English peer. Very important to the long-term prosperity of the Department. He's been looking for ranching prospects with a view to investment, as well as some hunting on the side." Swale paused now. Buckthorn was surprised by the worried look on his face. "His whole entourage dead?" he blurted.

Buckthorn nodded. "All of them apart from Mrs Fairfax," he affirmed. He felt he should add: "Same with the Galvos and the Marsdens."

To him, there wasn't an ace thickness of difference. Why all the damned fuss over Fairfax's party?

Swale still appeared stunned by the news. "Well, if true, the balloon will go up over this." His stone-grey stare fastened on to Buckthorn's steely gaze. "Are you sure?"

Buckthorn felt a hug of anger his word was doubted. "Damn it, I buried the man and his en-tour-rage as you call it."

"Where?" Swale's eyes were round, troubled, staring impatiently at him.

Buckthorn spat. "Back in the hills a piece."

Swales licked his dust-rimed lips. He seemed to pull himself together, bury his shocked surprise.

"Where is Lady Fairfax now? Is she well?"

Buckthorn chucked his head, indicating his rear again. "Down in the ravine with little Lucy Marsden. Fit enough, I guess."

Swale turned to the column, the supply mules behind, lined up halfway down the semi-arid slope falling away from the ravine towards brown, dry countryside. As if making an instant decision he waved his hand above his head with a circular movement. "Column ho-ooo." He indicated, bringing his arm horizontal, to the lip of the ravine. "This way, men."

Buckthorn followed Swale and trooper

Frame. The rattle of the hooves of their horses on the stony incline awakened Mrs Fairfax and brought her to her feet. Her green eyes stared up at them from under the ledge, clearly alarmed at first.

She relaxed visibly when she saw who they were.

Swale was brisk and correct. He dismounted and brought his white-gauntleted hand to a precise salute.

"Lady Fairfax," he said. "I am Lieutenant Swale, 5th Cavalry, Department of Arizona, out of Camp Sweeton." He smiled. "You are in good hands now, ma'am."

Buckthorn watched as she appraised Swale with those cool green eyes of hers. "Thank you, but I have been in 'good hands', as you say, from the moment Mr Buckthorn came to my rescue, Lieutenant," she said. "He has been a most excellent and courageous protector from then on."

Buckthorn breathed out silently with relief. Nothing about the spanking.

That would save a lot of explaining. But the courageous bit? He'd never live that down. Fact was there may be funny looks around the post from some quarters anyway. They'd better not let him see them.

He watched the smile fade from Swale's face at the compliment. "of course, Lady Fairfax," he said courteously. "Buckthorn is a conscientious scout, of proven ability, attached to the camp."

Swale seemed to fumble for words now. "Ma'am, may I say I regret very much what has happened to your ... to Lord Fairfax and his party. Buckthorn has informed me fully."

Buckthorn watched the woman's green eyes turned hard now, like emerald. "The murder of them is due entirely to our being most profoundly misled by your Department, Lieutenant. We were assured the natives were peaceful."

Swale seemed flustered by that. "And indeed they were, Lady Fairfax. This latest business was completely unforeseen. Your plight because of it is most regrettable."

Mrs Fairfax's chin came up. It was clear to Buckthorn the woman was in her element now, her grief under control. "Regrettable is too small a word, Lieutenant Swale," she said her voice evenly modulated. "Blundering gross incompetence by your Department would be better ones."

Swale's smile disappeared completely. He coughed and coloured. It was clear to Buckthorn the lieutenant didn't like what the woman said.

Swale shuffled. "On behalf of us all at Camp Sweeton," he said evenly, "may I offer my sincerest condolences and my regret we didn't reach you in time. My orders were to find your party and escort you to Camp Sweeton."

Mrs Fairfax's face remained stiff, tight, the eyes narrow, hard and bold. "Lamentably late orders it seems."

Swale licked his lips, his stare narrow and stony. Clearly he didn't like the remarks about the Department. He seemed to be holding his anger with difficulty.

"Lady Fairfax, I don't know what to say except that I am deeply sorry."

With that Mrs Fairfax seemed to relent, too. Perhaps she sensed Swale's growing resentment, Buckthorn thought.

"Well, not your fault, Lieutenant," she said. "But rest assured I will see the whole matter will be thoroughly gone into in Washington, at the highest level. I shall not rest until it is brought to a satisfactory conclusion. Now, pray, take us to safety, sir."

Swale relaxed visibly and nodded his head slightly. "At your service, Lady Fairfax."

As he said it the rest of the column came over the ravine edge and down into its shallow bottom.

Suddenly, behind them, little Lucy Marsden began to cry. Buckthorn turned to see her standing under the rock ledge — a lonely, desolate figure. She seemed to have just woken up.

Immediately Mrs Fairfax went to her, muttering soothing words and took her in her arms.

Swale followed her, erect and stiff. "I could get a trooper to take charge of the infant, ma'am," he offered tentatively. "We have family men in the patrol."

Mrs Fairfax turned, her eyes wide. "That won't be necessary, Lieutenant Swale," she said calmly, as if surprised. "Already Lucy and I are firm friends."

Swale nodded, looked relieved by her answer. "As you wish."

Swale now turned. Buckthorn met his hard gaze. "See me in ten minutes, Linus."

He went off giving orders. Seemed he'd decided to make camp.

★ ★ ★

Fifteen minutes later Swale now stared at Buckthorn over his coffee cup. All around the troopers busied themselves setting up camp.

"What do you think?" Swale said.

"Have you orders to engage?"

Swale shook his head. "Only if forced to. Our firm order was to find Lord Fairfax's party and get them out safely at all costs. I guess that still applies, even though there's only Lady Fairfax left."

"Best if we travel at night, then," Buckthorn said. "I figure there must be at least forty hostiles roamin' the vicinity. I know for sure Broken Nose is amongst them."

Swale narrowed his eyes, clearly not happy with the news. "He's vindictive and daring. And he'll have supplies. He won't head for the mountains until it's made too hot for him. He'll want more plunder." Swale gritted his teeth, hammered his fist into his left hand. "Damn!"

Buckthorn smiled inside. "You want to get amongst them, huh, Harve?" he said. "Well, after what I've seen these past two days I'm right with you on that score, but I guess our priority must be, as you say . . . " He nodded significantly towards Mrs Fairfax who was playing with Lucy.

He studied Swale again: the square face, bushy, ginger sideburns, stone-grey eyes.

"Think the hostiles know about *you*?"

"Tomás said they are about," Swale informed him. "He's picking up sign frequently. Says he's sure they know."

Buckthorn narrowed his eyes. Tomás was a full blood White Mountain Apache scout attached to Camp Sweeton. He used his Mexican name in preference to his Apache one. He was a good scout, thoroughly loyal.

"Where is he?"

"Probing around."

"What does he think beyond that?"

"They'll attack us before we get back to Camp Sweeton," relayed Swale.

Buckthorn nodded. He found himself in complete accord.

"Broken Nose could muster enough men to really make it hot for us. Maybe that's what he's doin' right now. It sure would be a feather in his cap to take us out."

Swale eyed him. "I've half a mind to take him on, he growled. "But you know my orders." He glowered across at Mrs Fairfax, playing with Lucy. "Damn it, that woman has a sharp tongue," he complained. "God help those that come up against her. How've you lived with her, Linus?"

"With difficulty sometimes, Harve." Buckthorn allowed himself a smile. "But there are ways of clearing the air sometimes."

Swale looked at him sharply. "You got a secret, Linus?"

Buckthorn nodded. "And on this occasion, it stays with me."

He got up to tend to his horse just as Tomás moved like a shadow into the ravine.

Buckthorn stayed with Swale.

Tomás slid off his pinto. A squat, wiry man with a barrel chest. His left eye was slightly higher than the other. His gash-like mouth also curled up on the left side caused by a knife wound, giving him a permanent sneer. He carried the regulation Springfield rifle in his left hand. He had the red identification headband round his forehead and black locks.

Swale regarded him with pale eyes. "Well, Tomás?"

The Apache squatted on his haunches staring at Swale sat on a rock feet from him.

"See Broken Nose," he said in a deep voice. "He know about us for sure. He got big party. Maybe forty. He winding up for big one."

Swale's face lengthened. He scrubbed his sideburns with a large hand. "He got scouts out?"

"Sure."

"We got a chance, Tomás?"

The Apache scout shrugged. "Always chance."

"He well armed?"

Tomás nodded. "See plenty guns. Aravaipa been busy in settlements. Plenty meat. Plenty horses."

Buckthorn realized Swale was looking at him. "Any ideas, Linus?"

"I don't think moving at night will help much now. Broken Nose can hit us when he likes. If we could get down to Crazy Man Creek . . . " Buckthorn paused, narrowed his eyes against the sun now resting on the lip of the ravine, slowly sinking below it. "He'll try and head us off, for sure. My guess is he'll try and get us in the passes on the run in to Camp Sweeton. Maybe he thinks we don't know he's on to us. Maybe he'll think we'll carry on into the fort by the used route. There we could surprise him. What we've got to do is not do what he thinks we'll do. That way we could dupe him and whup him."

Swale nodded, obviously interested. "Go on."

"There's an island, plumb in the middle of the creek at a wide point I know. It's built for defence. Lure him down to that and . . . "

Swale sucked at his bottom lip. "It's

risky," he said doubtfully. "And I have orders not to engage. He could wait us out. Starve us."

Tomás frowned, his face fierce. "He not time to wait too long; plenty soldiers soon come," he grunted. "Anyway, your orders no good. We in fix. Hit us in passes. Broken Nose got us over barrel. We have to fight."

Buckthorn cut in, "So we pick our ground. Crazy Man Creek." He looked hard at Swale.

The lieutenent was still sucking at his lip. "We could still use your first idea — night travel," he argued. "Perhaps we could lose him."

"If lose him, he still have lookout all down trail," Tomás grunted. "Use smoke. He get at us some way."

Swale got up. His broad brow was creased in thought. He paced backwards and forwards playing with his hands behind his back.

Finally he stopped and looked at them both. "Thank you both for your contribution. But I have my orders.

We'll try and outrun him."

"Harve . . . " Buckthorn started. They both knew it was a non-starter.

"That's orders, Linus!"

Buckthorn spat. Orders were made to wipe your backside on, he thought. What he knew of them anyway.

Tomás growled. "Damned orders. Damned orders no damned good here."

"Scout!" Swale rapped.

"What good scout if white eye not listen?"

Tomás went grumbling off.

One of the lookouts came down over the rimrock. He went straight up to Swale. "Seen dust on the far ridge, sir."

Buckthorn caught Swale's quick, hard stare. "Looks like Broken Nose is announcing himself," he said.

"Could be anything," Swale countered. "Wind. An animal."

"Harve, you don't convince me," Buckthorn returned.

Swale glared at him. "The order still sticks, damn it."

He stomped off to supervise supper.

Buckthorn looked across at little Lucy and Mrs Fairfax. Meeting the column, he began to think, maybe wasn't the best thing that had happened to him today. But that was the way it was, like it or not.

8

SUPPER had been eaten quietly. Now Buckthorn could almost touch the prickly tautness pervading the column as they filed out of the ravine into the dark Arizona night.

He had managed to acquire a spare bridle for his roan, had fitted it and had thrown away the rope makeshift.

Mrs Fairfax was mounted on the bay, pale and erect. Lucy was astride the saddle in front of her, wide awake, her brown eyes round and staring at the hard, grim cavalrymen around her.

Buckthorn couldn't help but doubt the wisdom of what Swale had elected to do. It was exactly — as Tomás and himself had insisted — what Broken Nose would expect, as sure as God made little apples.

And Buckthorn felt he could confidently bet dollars that the showing of dust before sunset was a ploy to make the column nervous as well; cause Swale to perhaps act recklessly in an effort to get back to Camp Sweeton.

Though Swale wouldn't be spooked like that, Buckthorn knew. He was a tough, experienced officer with courage. Buckthorn decided Swale genuinely thought his option was the better one.

Tomás melted into the night, towards the bluffs above which the banners of dust had been seen. Buckthorn moved up alongside Swale.

"Like to probe around a little, too, Harve," he said.

In the pale starlight Swale had met his stare with steady eyes. He nodded. "If you think it'll do any good."

Buckthorn eased the roan away south-west. He was interested to find out if Broken Nose had any braves on their left flank.

Soon the ground broke up, became hilly. He knew the land; had travelled it several times over the years. Ambush country, as was the run in to Camp

Sweeton. As was, he thought grimly, most of the country around here. That's what gave the Apache the edge. That and the Mexican border. And they could run up and down these rocky wastes like goats, with or without a horse.

He'd gone maybe three miles before he saw what he was hoping to see. He could just detect it. The faintest of glows. He guessed a lot of men would have missed it, not knowing what to look for. And it was over the next hillock.

He dismounted and ground-hitched the roan. She would stand. She had been taught. He paused halfway up the slope to wipe away the sweat moistening his brow. Now he licked his dry lips. No matter how often he did this he could never quite control the gut-tingling excitement and sometimes cold, wet-palm fear it aroused.

At the top of the rise he peered over. A rocky defile. Silhouetted in the faint fireglow he could see the braves were eating. Small, tough men, well-armed.

Using the faint light, he counted fifteen etched palely in its light.

Seemed Broken Nose intended to come in on them from both sides.

Buckthorn looked further now. In the light of the pale moon that had risen, he could see horses bunched up lower down the narrow pass.

He crept along just below the top of the defile to get a better look. When he looked again he found two boys were standing guard.

He blinked. If he could set the horses running . . .

He found his mind was now working fast, along with his probing gaze. He could come in from the west end of the defile. If he was careful enough he could take them completely by surprise. It was obvious they weren't expecting anything to disturb their meal.

His mind started to warm to the plan. He could set the horses running up the defile; drive them right through the camp. It would cause chaos and maybe kick a few of the red heathen to death into the bargain. At the very least, it would slow this bunch down considerably; weaken Broken Nose's plan of attack, maybe even destroy it completely.

Buckthorn found his whole body was now humming like a spinning top with the anticipation of it. He wanted like hell to bring the plan he had devised to fruition now.

Exhilarated he eased back down the slope to his roan.

But instantly, as he got near, he could see the horse was restless, flicking its ears and chucking its head. Alerted by it Buckthorn narrowed his eyes and looked around him. Nothing he could see. But he found his senses keening up. He proceeded with much more caution now. Maybe it was just some critter nearby that had disturbed her, he thought, but he couldn't take that chance.

He'd got his hands almost on to the saddle on the roan when the attack came, silent and swift. He was only aware from which direction it was coming at the last, desperate moment. The hiss of a moccasin on rough rock behind him.

He spun, hoisting his skinning knife, the wooden haft familiar in his hand. He was quick enough to parry away the thrust to his stomach, but even so he felt the Apache's blade skidding with sharp pain across his ribs.

Seeing the Aravaipa's rush and miss had thrown him off-balance, Buckthorn reacted with lightning speed.

Knife aloft he followed up, pacing over the ground between them swiftly. With brutal savagery he drove the blade into the brave's back. The Apache's harsh cry filled the night with sudden noise.

Buckthorn cursed. That was the last thing he wanted. He tried to pull the knife out with a fierce jerk. But it resisted, the flesh sucking at it. It needed a twist. To his relief it came.

The buck was still screaming a warning.

Leaving the brave writhing where he lay, Buckthorn swung up into the saddle. As he did so the first Aravaipa topped the crest of the hill above him. Buckthorn saw him silhouetted in the pale moonlight.

He put the roan into a run, off into the night, his hair prickling up as the sound of three arrows, hissing past him into the silver dark ahead, came in quick succession.

Now he was cursing himself. Damn it he should have known. They were bound to have had somebody watching. He was supposed to know his business! With a little more care and a little more stealth he could have turned this whole business on its head; given the column the advantage. Now the chance had been missed and the Apaches would be even more riled up, losing a man that way.

* * *

Back with the column an hour later Swale shrugged in the saddle beside Buckthorn after he had related the story. "Well, it's done," he said. "At least he knows he's got a fight on his hands. And, further, we now know he's going to come at us from both sides."

Buckthorn scrubbed his two-day beard. "Maybe not now," he offered. "Now he knows *we* know."

"I've been thinking about your Crazy Man Creek idea," Swale said now. "You really think it would work?"

Perking up, quietly elated to hear Swale hadn't completely abandoned his plan, Buckthorn nodded.

"It's the best option we have," he said. "It would draw Broken Nose off the trail to Camp Sweeton, allow you to send a rider to the camp for help."

Swale was very interested now. "Who?"

"Tomás," Buckthorn said immediately. "If anybody can do it, he can. There is another thing, too: if we followed Crazy Man Creek to come into the fort from that direction, instead of the passes, Broken Nose'd take little bits off us all the way down and swallow the last mouthful before we reached Camp Sweeton. We can't even follow the river route. Too many bluffs each side. It'd be like a turkey shoot."

Swale was pulling at his sideburns now. He went quiet, clearly thinking. After seconds he nodded and said, "I agree with you, there is little chance for us if we take the normal trail into Camp Sweeton. We'd be cut to ribbons in the passes. And the lie of the land across the river is unfriendly to cavalry work."

Buckthorn heard Swale growl frustratedly in the night beside him. "What a damned infernal country this is," he snorted. "And what a damned place to stick a fort!"

★ ★ ★

Halting to rest the horses intermittently throughout the night dawn found the column at breakfast.

Buckthorn knew that Crazy Man Creek lay to the west of them, about six miles.

As he sat scooping up beans with a hunk of dark, hard bread Tomás rode in.

The squat White Mountain Apache moved to him and stared at him after he had dismounted and helped himself to food. "Big commotion two hour before dawn at Broken Nose camp. Something happened in night."

Buckthorn turned a steel-grey eye upon the scout. "Maybe me, Tomás," he said.

He told what had happened.

Tomás nodded gravely. "Caused damn big stir."

But now the barrel-chested Apache threw back his head and set to laughing. Because he did, his flat, twisted face almost made him look as if he was in pain.

"You cock ass at Broken Nose, eh, Linus Buckthorn?" he chortled. You cock ass."

Buckthorn grinned back, wryly; but he surely didn't see it that way. He was damned mad about it.

"Nearly cocked toes, Tomás," he quipped.

That set the scout off into further squawks of laughter.

Swale came over, staring at the scout, as if puzzled and surprised the usually dour Apache could laugh. "What you got, Tomás?" he said, not bothering to ask about the hilarity.

The laughter subsided. Tomás's eyes went black, narrow and fierce again. "Broken Nose going to come pretty soon. He heading to cut you off. He know now, pretty good, that you know. Linus Buckthorn see to that — and dust last night his signal too."

Buckthorn caught Swale's brief glance. He was a little surprised the lieutenant didn't comment on the opinion.

Instead he said, "We're going to try

161

the Crazy Man Creek idea, Tomás."

The Apache grinned exposing his yellow, uneven teeth. "One big bloody fight, eh? We whip them." He drew his hand across his throat. "Whip them good."

Swale looked at the Indian steadily. "You're going to ride into Camp Sweeton for help, Tomás," he said. "We could maybe wrap this up if we hit him from both sides."

Tomás lost his humour. He went sober-looking, stone-faced. "Broken Nose," he said gravely, "he not fool. He clever man. He'll have lookout on trail. Tomás maybe not get through."

Swale's face set grimly. "Then you'll have to be careful."

Tomás looked disappointed. "I want fight. Long time, no fight."

"The ride to the fort will take more courage, Tomás," Swale said. "I want my best man to do it."

Tomás was still grave-faced. "Broken Nose. He watch. All time." Then he suddenly grinned, his face lighting up.

He tapped his head. "But Tomás think better. White Mountain Indian better than ten Aravaipa."

Swale smiled. "Don't you think I didn't have that in mind when I asked you?" he said.

The scout's chest swelled. He grinned again. "Sure. I knew that. All time. Just kidding." He turned. "Eat now." He started scooping food off his plate.

Meanwhile Buckthorn was scanning the hills east. He could see smoke.

He turned his eyes south-west. More smoke, rising into the cobalt sky.

"They're talking," he said to Swale and indicated with his right arm.

Swale followed his point, his square face looking fatigued through lack of sleep. "Yeah," he breathed. "I guess the sooner we reach Crazy Man Creek the better." The lieutenant pulled at his sideburns now. "I want to skirt as close to the hills as possible before turning for the river. I want to run the bluff at the last minute. I want to get in a position where Tomás can slip away without being seen. I want to keep Broken Nose guessing."

Buckthorn nodded. "Keeping close to the hills could maybe do it," he contributed. "Give us time to get down there and dig in."

Swale stared at him now. "You sure this island you're talking about is as defendable as you make out?"

Buckthorn stared at him. "It's my neck on the line too, remember." There was another thing, Buckthorn now thought. "What rations have you got?"

Swale's stone-grey eyes met Buckthorn's quizzical stare. The look seemed slightly evasive, as if he didn't want to disclose something. "We left with enough for a week."

"How long have you been on the trail?"

"Two days." Swale gestured with a cut of his hand. "Damn it we lost a mule in Nailer Pass. Snake spooked it. Lost its footing and dropped a hundred feet into the river. It took three days' vittles with it."

That focused Buckthorn's look sharply. "Meaning we've only got two days' food left?"

Swale nodded. He grunted a sort of frustrated sigh. "We'll just have to tighten up. If Camp Sweeton responds quickly it should be enough."

Buckthorn looked up. The sun was now well up. He lowered his gaze now. To the west the smoke had stopped.

Then he turned to meet Swale's steady stare. The lieutenant sighed. "Well, guess we'd better get the show on the road, Linus."

Buckthorn watched Swale move away to talk to Sergeant Bushy. He thought it's just one damned annoyance after another. He'd never known things to take such a bad turn.

9

BY mid-morning the sun was hot enough to fry eggs. The gentle breeze fanned searing heat across Buckthorn's lantern-jawed, lean, deeply-tanned face. Occasionally he looked at Mrs Fairfax riding in the middle of the column, Lucy on the saddle in front of her. Her proud, haughty face was shaded by the hat he had found for her at her husband's ravaged camp. He spat and narrowed his eyes. That seemed a long time ago now.

Since they broke camp he had watched the Apache smoke become more active again. Then a group of about thirty Aravaipa showed themselves.

They appeared suddenly. They rode about a mile away, along the top of a broken ridge to the north-east. Their dust was swirling skyward, borne on the furnace-hot gusts of air. He noticed Mrs Fairfax was staring at them defiantly, hugging Lucy closer to her.

The Apache stayed for a half-hour or more. The whole column watched them with hard, keen eyes. Then, as quickly as they had appeared, they melted into the hot brown landscape again.

Seeing it, Tomás broke from the column. Within seconds he was lost in the burning hills. Now Buckthorn caught Swale's hard stare as he turned to him. Through dust-rimed lips Swale said, "Take us to the river, Linus!"

Buckthorn nodded and put himself in the lead while Swale told the men to follow him. That done, Buckthorn set his lips in a grim line. He urged the roan into a long stride.

The men pushed up the gait of their mounts to pace with him. Tobacco juice was spat. Lean, hard faces were lengthened. Springfield rifles were lovingly caressed. Keen eyes peered warily at the tortured, shimmering country around.

Buckthorn led the column down the long, winding defile towards the river, which took them out of the edge of the foothills.

Buckthorn let his restless gaze search the skyline each side constantly. There was the band he had encountered last night. They would be the ones to watch for, he had no doubt. Unless the smoke had sent a different message, they would still be on their flank.

As they came out of the defile, he saw the creek. A silver ribbon under the white-hot sky. Looking north, maybe a mile and a half away, Buckthorn could see the island they were heading for.

Here the tall bluffs stood off maybe half a mile away from the river. They stepped redly down to a fringe of loose rocks before dipping their toes in the sluggish, broad creek. Trees and brush greened its banks before melding into the arid, orange-brown country spreading away each side.

Buckthorn knew the island was fairly large. It would take the column and its horses with room to spare. There was plenty of cover. Driftwood was beached on it; tall brush grew there; several trees, mostly shimmering-leafed aspens. There were also boulders.

Now a string of Apaches streamed out of the bluffs half a mile from them to the south. They vomited towards them like a running, pus-filled sore, dust clouding up behind them.

It must be the bunch he had tangled with last night, Buckthorn decided. Now he swung his gaze in the other direction. He was not surprised to see, to the north-west, the rest of Broken Nose's gathered force reveal themselves again.

Buckthorn swallowed on a dry throat. And they had been underestimated. There were more than fifty braves coming in on them like the closing jaws of a nutcracker.

Oddly the island seemed to be some kind of haven to him now. A thing to go for in an impossible world. It was nonsense, Buckthorn recognized. Yet it would be reasonably cool, the creek being melt-water from the mountains. And it could be defended well.

By the time they were splashing through the water that was belly-deep in the middle, the band south had closed in to a quarter of a mile.

Splashing up out of the creek on to the island Buckthorn could hear Swale rapping orders.

Urgently Buckthorn drew up alongside Mrs Fairfax. "Dismount, ma'am," he bawled.

He swung out of leather and assisted her with Lucy, holding the roan by the rein. A trooper took it and Mrs Fairfax's bay and led them to the centre of the island. Four troopers were holding the rest of the column's mounts.

Blanket and Winchester in one hand, Lucy held in the other, Buckthorn stared at Mrs Fairfax. He could see her face was taut with excitement, the green eyes bright. There was no fear there; apprehension for the unknown, maybe.

"Follow me, Mrs Fairfax," he rapped.

His eyes searched for a spot where he could defend them. Why did he want to defend them, they weren't kin? he thought suddenly, ridiculously. He found he couldn't answer himself articulately. Maybe for little Lucy? Or just the inborn urge in some men to defend the womenfolk.

He spotted a big, gnarled, bone-white bole of timber that had been pushed a dozen yards from the water's edge by flood water.

"Take Lucy and lay flat against it," he ordered, looking at the woman. She nodded, didn't answer him, just did what he asked.

Now he wrapped the blanket around his stomach. It was an old Mexican trick he'd learned from them for fighting Apaches. They knew from long experience, the Apache always aimed his arrows at the stomach.

That accomplished Buckthorn threw himself down behind the tree bole and peered at the river. Already a phalanx of barrel-chested ponies with fearsome, painted Aravaipas on their backs were white-watering into the creek. Soon the belly-deep water slowed them down.

"Hold your fire," rapped Swale. "Wait for the command!" Buckthorn could see the lieutenant was knelt on one knee, his Colt in his hand.

Buckthorn licked his lips. The Aravaipa were within thirty yards now. Damned close. Damn it, give the command, Swale, his thoughts urged. Lead and arrows were already buzzing around them, too close for comfort.

"Fire at will!" roared Swale, suddenly.

The volley rattled out and Buckthorn saw red death visit the braves. Four dropped, two swayed and hung on. The water began churning as the Apaches made frantic attempts to disperse. The river became crimson with blood.

Whooping now the Apaches spread, bringing their own rifles into action.

Another volley rang out from the island, followed by staccato rifle fire. The firing started to swell up to a roaring cacophony, rebounding echoes through the serried hills around like rampaging thunder.

Buckthorn fired coolly, deliberately. However he found it was getting difficult to see through the thickening, acrid clouds of powder smoke belching from some forty guns.

With shocking suddenness the brave came at him from nowhere, bursting through the gunsmoke haze. Buckthorn only had time to whack him off his horse with the butt of his Winchester as he hung down to swipe him with his tomahawk.

Buckthorn switched the Winchester to fire position now. Vaguely he could hear Lucy screaming to his left.

He pulped the brave's face with a close-range shot. The Apache rolled twice before crashing into bushes. He was obviously dead.

Then, as suddenly as it had started,

the melee was over.

The whoops of the braves were receding. The powder smoke was drifting slowly away down-river to reveal the Apache running up out of the river on to the far, rising bank, carrying what wounded and dead they could reach with them.

Back against the tree bole again Buckthorn watched and waited.

Ten minutes later a party of about twenty braves broke cover, three hundred yards up-river. The disturbed water glistened in the harsh, overhead sun as they splashed across the creek.

It had to come, Buckthorn thought bleakly.

While the column waited, watching the move, Swale ordered the water canteens to be filled before their rear was covered. Buckthorn could hear him redeploying the men, too.

Mrs Fairfax got up and crossed to Lieutenant Swale. They talked for moments before Swale went to one of the pack mules. He pulled out a

Springfield rifle and handed it to her along with a handful of cartridges.

Buckthorn blinked. Well, no matter where the woman had come from, wherever it was, they sure bred them tough, he had to concede.

She came back to the tree bole and settled down, resting the rifle barrel on the timber. She stared at him.

"I'm curious, Mr Buckthorn." She wiggled her right index finger in a slightly imperious way. "Why the blanket?"

He told her.

"How fascinating," she said.

Calm as a mountain pool, he thought. There had to be some nerve to jerk at somewhere and he had to know.

"You afraid, ma'am?"

"Frankly, I'm petrified," she said. "I'm shivering like a jelly. But one has to try and control that sort of thing."

The hell you do, he thought.

Two shots snapped across the water from where the first attack had come from and he crouched down. Now whoops came shrilly. And this time they came from both sides.

"Hold your fire, men," called Swale. "Make every shot count. Fire at my command."

Again he let them come on until Buckthorn could see the Apaches' painted faces clearly. Then his heart missed a beat when his steely gaze found Broken Nose.

Alerted, he stiffened. With calm calculation he drew a bead right on the blue shirted chest of the Apache plunging his piebald through the water towards them. He knew if he put Broken Nose out of the fight things could change mighty rapidly.

"Fire at will!" bawled Swale.

Buckthorn cursed as the brave cut in front of his line right at the crucial moment. Buckthorn saw his lead hit him, sending him sideways out of the saddle. The buck splashed with a cry into the creek. But Broken Nose was still on his horse his Winchester up and firing, his visage savage behind it.

Braves were riding everywhere now, crisscrossing, whooping and firing. But Buckthorn knew the one best chance he'd had had gone.

Lead was humming with vicious noise and light, seemingly flimsy barbed arrows were flying along their deadly paths. A few war lances arced over, too.

Again the gunsmoke began to haze things. If only there was more breeze, damn it, Buckthorn thought.

He fired frantically at a charging buck, knocking the Indian's horse out from under him. The brave took Buckthorn's next shot which knocked him back into the deep water to disappear, only to surface lower down in the slow current, swimming weakly.

A charging Aravaipa came out of the smoke. Buckthorn could not avoid being bowled over as the pony hit him a glancing blow. The Apache brought his mount to a skidding stop and turned his six-gun on Buckthorn.

The crash of a Springfield, almost in his ear, deafened Buckthorn for moments as he was swinging his Winchester up, he knew too late.

The buck smashed back out of his blanket saddle. A big red hole appeared in his chest, blood spurting out.

Buckthorn turned slightly surprised eyes to find his saviour. For as sure as hell the Apache had had him dead to rights. It was Mrs Fairfax, busy reloading the singleshot.

He would hand her his thanks late —

He took the buck mid-air as he came running out of the bushes on his pinto and leaping from his blanket saddle. In his desperation to hold the buck off, Buckthorn had to drop the Winchester.

He went staggering back into the water driven there by the impact of the flying Apache.

He could see the tomahawk swinging into a position to strike him. Gasping his anxiety, his lips drawn tight against his clenched teeth, Buckthorn pulled his Remington New Army cleanly. The report was a crisp, snapping boom as he squeezed off.

The buck's chin disappeared in a bloody mess. Blood gouted out. Buckthorn drove his next shot into the Apache's brain.

Gunsmoke was stinging his eyes and leaving a bad taste in his mouth now. He glared round madly.

But the fighting went off the boil, as swiftly as it had flared up. Again, as the smoke drifted away, Buckthorn could see the Apaches heading back to the creek banks.

Then he noticed something that could pay off dividends: the bank across at the rear of the island. It was piled rocks in front, then a sheer face of what looked loose rock behind. The Aravaipa had taken cover between the two.

Buckthorn narrowed his eyes. Well, well . . .

He turned to Mrs Fairfax however. "Ma'am, I guess we're even," he said.

She smiled, eyes bright with battle

fever, despite having a slight graze on her neck. He could see her face, too, was grimed with black powder and running with sweat in the now fierce afternoon heat.

"As you say in your vernacular, Mr Buckthorn, I guess we are."

Then the woman turned to comfort Lucy who was huddled against the tree bole shivering and weeping.

Buckthorn smiled to himself and looked round. He didn't know what the hell the word 'vernacular' meant but it sure sounded swell. And thanks to the ample cover on the island, he saw the casualties amongst the troopers was light. Two dead, three with serious wounds.

Seeing the wounded men, Mrs Fairfax went to their aid immediately, leaving Lucy with a trooper. It became obvious to Buckthorn she knew quite a bit about medical matters and soon had the wounded men as comfortable as it was possible under field conditions. In two cases she administered laudanum, found in the field medical box.

Now Buckthorn went to Lieutenant Swale. He showed him the crumbling cliff at the back of the Apaches across on the other bank.

Swale nodded gravely, his grey eyes studying him. "What you got in mind, Linus?"

"With a keg of powder, I could make a hell of a mess of those heathens over there," he said.

"You'd never get near them," Swale dismissed.

"Give me a good man and a keg of gunpowder and a length of fuse, I'll dispute that."

Swale looked at him more seriously. "Damn it, Linus," he said. "You don't have to. We're in a pretty strong position here. Broken Nose has taken more casualties than he'll admit to. We just have to face it out and wait for the column from Camp Sweeton."

"I think the harder we hit Broken Nose the quicker he'll break off," insisted Buckthorn. "They don't like takin' too many casualties. There ain't enough of them. They like to hit and run. That's what they're most good at. He'll begin to think that the guns and glory he'll achieve here'll be worth less than the lives of his bucks."

Swale was clearly turning over what Buckthorn had said in his mind. Then he compressed his lips as he reached his decision. "We'll wait for the column from Sweeton," he said.

"Suppose it don't come?" pursued Buckthorn. "You ain't got the food to sustain a long siege."

Again Swale looked at him thoughtfully. "Don't think I'm not grateful for ideas, Linus. I promise to keep it in mind."

With that he turned and went amongst the men, detailing strategy and ordering more ammunition to be distributed.

★ ★ ★

Buckthorn stared up at the brassy, late afternoon sky. The heat sucked a man inside out, despite the welcome coolness of the water around them.

Nothing had happened since the two furious attacks at noon, apart from long range sniping on the part of the Aravaipa, with few results. One bullet had grazed a trooper across the chest, nothing more.

But it was still uncomfortable, Buckthorn decided. A man had to move with great caution. However, behind makeshift protection, a meal of sorts had been cooked. Beans, coffee and hard biscuits was better then nothing. Very welcome, in fact.

Hunched over his plate, sat on a tree bole, Swale said, "Do you think they'll attack under cover of the dark?"

Buckthorn pursed his lips. "They don't like to," he said. "They think if they do get killed, their soul will get lost in the blackness and they won't make it to the Happy Hunting Ground. But they've been known to do it in bright moonlight. And they ain't averse to picking off strays when there ain't much danger to them."

Then a hell of a commotion started up on the side of the river Buckthorn knew Broken Nose to be on. Shouting and whooping.

Then a trooper came close to Swale and pointed. "Down by the river, sir," he said.

Swale got up and put his tin plate down on the log. Buckthorn rose with him and they crept to the edge of the island.

Two bucks were sat their mounts at the water's edge. The rest were lined up on the bluff above. Between the two at the edge of the water was Tomás.

Buckthorn narrowed his eyes. Or what was left of him . . . The scout's head was sunk down on his chest. His naked body was covered in blood. Buckthorn knew the Apache were expert at keeping a man alive to prolong his torture and agony for days if they saw fit.

Now Buckthorn picked out the Spanish that was being bawled across the water at them.

In essence it was saying, Tomás no good White Mountain bastard, puppy to white eye. No help from Camp Sweeton for Buckthorn now, or *capitan* horse soldier Swale. All white eyes die now.

A great series of whoops and calls came from the lined-up Aravaipas.

Swale's face was grave and hollow as he turned to Buckthorn.

But Buckthorn rose, ignoring him, a cold rage churning in him. He'd ridden many a long trail with Tomás.

He adjusted the backsight of his Winchester with deliberate, calm intent. Damned if he was going to let this one lie.

He had the range right.

At the light pressure of his finger the Winchester kicked back into his shoulder. Almost immediately there was a harsh yell from the brave to Tombs's left. He keeled out of his blanket saddle. He flopped on to the red mud of the bank.

As Buckthorn jacked in another cartridge the other brave whooped and blew Tomás's brains out, ending the White Mountain's agony. Now the Apache turned his pinto and kicked for the bluff, still yelling defiance.

Buckthorn swung the Winchester again. He felt cold. Deliberate. He'd force no urgency on to himself here.

He squeezed off. Again the Winchester roared. The brave swayed, but didn't fall and Buckthorn cursed as the Aravaipa reached cover.

Now a rash of firing started up before the Aravaipas melted back of the top of the bluff.

"Cease firing!" Swale bawled. "Save your lead for a target you can hit!"

The shooting died down. A few defiant shots came from the Aravaipas, then silence came save for the echoes ringing into the hills.

"He knows he can wait now," Buckthorn said harshly, turning to the lieutenant. He held Swale's stone-grey stare. "What about that gunpowder, Harve?"

Swale beat a hard right fist on to his left hand. "Damn it, Linus," he growled. "It's hare-brained. I can't ask you to take such a risk. There's no guarantee it will work."

Buckthorn narrowed his eyelids. "You ain't asking me," he said. "I'm asking you."

"But it'll have to be my decision," rapped Swale irritably.

Buckthorn held the lieutenant's probing stare. "Then make it," he said.

Swale shuffled. Buckthorn met the lieutenant's bright glare, flaring with momentary anger. He resented his curt demand, Buckthorn realized, but he also knew Swale knew he would have to go for it.

Swale firmed his jaw. He nodded quickly.

"Pick your man," he grated. "I'll find you powder."

10

IT was now dark. About Buckthorn the night air had a cool velvet feel about it.

With a steely gaze he stared around him in the gloom. The moon had yet to rise. If the Apaches were going to skirmish, they wouldn't do it yet, he judged.

Beside him Trooper Hank Simmons was crouched in the gently lapping water. He'd picked Simmons because he knew him. Knew he was cool under fire and not easily scared. And he knew how to move quiet.

With one hand Buckthorn held the small, crude raft they had constructed. On that was the keg of gunpowder and a rope of fuse.

Swale stood in the water beside them. His stare was serious and stern. Well, good luck, Linus . . . Trooper Simmons."

Buckthorn nodded. Simmons mumbled, "Yo."

With a last look around the white, tense faces on the island, with Simmons Buckthorn slid out into the deeper water holding the raft in front of him and allowed the current to take them downstream.

On each side of the creek Buckthorn could hear the Apache drums banging, see the fires glowing. He listened to the wild songs being sung.

He found the gentle lap of the water around him was lulling. It was inky black where the faint yellow glow of the Apache fires didn't catch it. Buckthorn realized the rocking movement was lulling him into a cool, quiet calm. A false sense of a peace. And a mile downstream he had to force himself to snap out if it. Now, with Simmons, he turned the raft for the shore, towards the dark clump of aspen there.

They came up out of the water with hardly a splash and Simmons hefted the gunpowder. Buckthorn took the fuse. Stealthily they moved up the eroding bluffs.

Buckthorn had spent some time during the afternoon studying the rocks with his binoculars. He had found it was less vertical here. He had observed the scarp ledged up in steps of crumbling rock.

He proceeded with tentative, cat-like caution now, Simmons stepping as silently as himself behind him.

On the flatter rock at the top, Buckthorn took the keg of gunpowder.

He moved forward with infinite patience, pausing frequently to stare into the night around, listen to it. Ahead and below him he could see the fires and the shadows of the dancing men like spiders on the red walls.

As he and Simmons drew closer he could see the braves were having a fine old hoe-down, Apache style. They were hyping up for the big one tomorrow, was his immediate thought. He allowed himself a grim smile. He didn't feel at all sorry about having to disappoint them.

At the top of the sheer bluff, rising out of the rubble below, Buckthorn could see the Apaches clearly. They were drumming and dancing on the narrow strip of flat ground before the next mound of rocks, which screened them from the island and also acted as a breastworks.

Buckthorn glanced at the bulk of land in the middle of the creek; the island. It was just a very dark shape, hardly discernible in the starlight. It had a strange sort of serenity about it. But Buckthorn knew there was a lot of apprehension there, a lot of fearful watchfulness. And he also knew there was a sackful of raw guts there, too, ready to meet anything thrown at it.

Now his keen gaze searched for lookouts. There was nothing on the bluff top. Then, on a ledge twenty feet above the dancing braves, Buckthorn spotted one watchman. On the rocks screening them from the island, he could see three more were spaced out along it.

He stared at Simmons. The trooper was stood tall and patient beside him, the coil of fuse over his arm. His face was pale and hollow in the faint light from the fires below. But it was determined.

Buckthorn pointed to a large bulk of rock poised over the dancing braves below. It was riven with deep cracks. It just needed a hefty jolt and . . .

Simmons licked his lips, nodded, understanding him. Buckthorn blinked and stared into the darkness. No point in waiting, he thought.

Now he felt the cold clamminess of his wet buckskins, and he found it was decidedly cooler on the top of these red scarps. But he felt warm inside with suppressed excitement.

He bent. Hardly daring to breathe, he crept forward, the keg cradled in his strong, sinewy arms. With a hard, alert gaze he searched for seconds before he found the most effective place to put the charge.

Once he had found it, he made a

hollow to take it, in a position where it would push tons of the red rock down on the dancing Aravaipas.

He took out the bung and pushed in the fuse, plugging the hole again with rag. He moistened his lips. They had become extremely dry. With care he paced back, unwinding the fuse. Its length took them a good twenty feet from the keg of gunpowder.

The end reached, Buckthorn stared at Simmons who stood tight-lipped and tense next to him.

Buckthorn knew words weren't needed. He fumbled out the waterproof package he had wrapped his sulphur matches in. With a slightly shaking hand he scraped one on a rock and held it to the fuse.

It spluttered into life and began to run sparkling along the black snake leading to the keg. With Simmons, Buckthorn ran to the shelter of rocks nearby.

And waited.

Buckthorn watched the trace of

twinkling yellow fire run along the ground, smoke weaving from it. Then came the horrendous, crashing detonation accompanied with orange-yellow flashes of flames. Billowing black smoke and dust writhed into the sky.

The bluff top seemed to spring into the air, tremble, then shudder down the side of the sheer hillside into the campfire-lit night below. A rain of huge boulders went bouncing and crashing down.

Buckthorn, alive with anticipation, ran to the edge of the bluff. The lead rocks were already thundering into the dancing Aravaipas. Already harsh cries of pain came, killing the chanting.

But Buckthorn stared down dispassionately. He could see bodies were already being smashed into bloody pulps. He could see few would escape the fearsome deluge of rock. Then, all of a sudden, as though a light had been snuffed out, the whole terrible scene was buried under piles of rock and earth.

Buckthorn knew there could be little life left under it.

He could see dust was billowing up. It came chokingly out of the blackness, gritty to the teeth. Buckthorn spat it out.

A breathless quiet closed down on the night. Only the echoes of the explosion rolled distantly through the hills across the river. Buckthorn thought the night had suspended itself for moments, in disbelief.

Across the creek the chanting of the other Aravaipas had stopped. The only sound to split the night air again was a whooping 'Yeeeehaaaah' from the island. Then it, too, went silent, as if in awe.

Buckthorn recovered himself quickly. With a swift look at Simmons, he said, "Let's go, Hank."

Simmons nodded and spat and moved his chaw.

Buckthorn reckoned he could read it in Hank's face what the trooper thought of the business. Though not especially liking what had been done, he was a soldier. He had done his job. It could be him down there. Maybe tomorrow it would be his turn to lie staring sightless at the sun, with an Apache war arrow deep in his gut.

Buckthorn blinked at the darkness. It remained to be seen what Broken Nose would do about their night's work . . .

* * *

The early morning sun painted the bluffs west with raw light. It ran like blood down the riven earth and rock to sprinkle and sparkle like diamonds on the creek.

Buckthorn stood with Swale on the island. They had listened to a different kind of chanting for the rest of the night from the Apache. A sorrowful, haunting sound.

Now they watched the Aravaipas start to file across the creek again from the destruction Buckthorn had done across the river.

There were several travois bearing braves. Pain and misery hung over their bowed heads like a shroud. Buckthorn rubbed his hawk-like nose. He spat. Hell, he thought. He felt, oddly, damned sorry about it.

Mrs Fairfax came up alongside him. He noticed she had washed her face and combed her hair. Little Lucy was as spruce and clean as circumstances would allow beside her. "I feel I want to cry, Linus," she said suddenly. "Those poor savages."

Linus . . . ?

Buckthorn looked at her. He could see the proud haughtiness in her had mellowed. There seemed a preparedness to accept other people had dignity and pride and rights . . . and first names. But beyond that, about the Apache, they always gave as good as they got. It wasn't over.

But he said, "They've taken a beating for sure, *Lady* Fairfax."

He noticed it was her turn to stare

at him, a small smile playing on her sensuous lips, as if enjoying his response. But before the conversation expanded Swale nudged his arm and pointed.

Buckthorn saw a lone rider cantering up from downstream. He could see it was Broken Nose, erect and proud on his piebald. Abruptly he stopped on the creek's edge across from them. With a slow, majestic movement he raised his hand-clasped Winchester above his head.

"We are The People, white eyes," he shouted. "You cannot kill us. We shall live forever on this land, either as dust, or as men." He lifted his head, his face fierce with pride in the warm sun. "One day *you* will be dust, but you will not belong here." He pointed his rifle to the red soil beneath him. "In this land only the Apache and his Mother are one."

He stopped and folded his arms proudly across his chest, his rifle cradled in them. "That is all Broken Nose has to say for now," he said. "His heart is heavy. At this moment he is tired of war."

With that he turned the piebald and put it up the steep side of the bluff and disappeared into the gold of the early sun.

Swale let out a deep sigh as he went. "Well, seems he's had enough and I haven't the strength to follow him and engage," he grunted. "We'll eat before we head for Camp Sweeton, Linus."

Buckthorn nodded.

"Yeah. Sure."

But now he stared across the river, at the body of the White Mountain scout still lying on the creek bank. The place where he had been put out of his misery yesterday. He noticed the dead Aravaipa had gone.

"Guess I'll go and get Tomás," he said. "Bury him decent."

Swale nodded. "Hell, why not?" he agreed. He went off bellowing orders.

And Buckthorn crossed the river.

Postscript

LADY AMANDA FAIRFAX went back to England. She took Lucy with her as her adopted daughter.

Lieutenant Harvey Swale fought several campaigns, was involved in the surrender of Geronimo to Nelson (Bear Coat) Miles and went on to become a captain. He died of drink twenty-five years later in a Chicago slum.

Later Broken Nose fought loyally alongside Victorio and Geronimo until captured. He died in Florida forty years later. His bones were returned to Arizona, by a white man who had befriended him. They were placed in the arms of Broken Nose's Earth Mother, overlooking Aravaipa Creek. The white man said the Apache had often talked about his homeland: always with great sadness.

In 1904 Buckthorn was shot four times by an unknown assailant in a dark side-street of a border town. He was buried penniless and without ceremony on Boothill.

He left no family.

No mark.

Other titles in the
Linford Western Library:

TOP HAND
Wade Everett

The Broken T was big. But no ranch is big enough to let a man hide from himself.

GUN WOLVES OF LOBO BASIN
Lee Floren

The Feud was a blood debt. When Smoke Talbot found the outlaws who gunned down his folks he aimed to nail their hide to the barn door.

SHOTGUN SHARKEY
Marshall Grover

The westbound coach carrying the indomitable Larry and Stretch headed for a shooting showdown.